Adam

1

He created them male and female, and blessed them and called them Mankind in the day they were created

Genesis 5:2

The Lord God planted a garden eastward in Eden, and there He put the man whom He had formed.

And out of the ground the Lord God made every tree grow that is pleasant to the sight and good for food.

Genesis 2:8-9

Eden is the greatest place ever. There are no laws, and we can do whatever we want. Of course, there are occasionally misunderstandings between people. Sometimes we get into scuffles. But that is nothing compared to all of the joy, fun and pleasure we have around here.

The weather is good. It rains sometimes, just enough to give us the water we need. The sky is usually sunny with a few fluffy clouds. There are forests and meadows, and many of the trees are fruit trees. We get all of the fruit and berries we want. There is also plenty of game to hunt and we feast on meat whenever we want it. There aren't too many predators to kill us humans; and whenever they come around we have pointy-tipped spears to keep them at bay. There's no such thing as responsibility. We have no need for it. Life is pretty easy for us. Everything we need is provided. If somebody does something wrong, there is no one to tell them they were wrong. The only consequence, sometimes, is that the person who was wronged wants revenge. But even when people kill each other in a fight, we know that it just comes with the territory. No one lives forever. We don't worry about what might happen, or how our end will come. We just enjoy ourselves and live well, and when it's time to go, it's time to go. No sweat.

We're all pretty easygoing at Eden. The only time anybody gets anxious is when they want something they really don't need. People like that are losers anyway. It's best to just want what you have, then you always have enough. And we have plenty here. No one is poor, no one is deprived. Everybody is pretty much equal. Not that we have much of a society. We pretty much live for ourselves. But if anyone gets sick, injured or old, there's always someone willing to throw them a bone and take care of them.

We have pretty comfortable shelters. Usually people build themselves tents or little huts, or they sleep in caves or just under the open sky. It's never too hot or too cold; the only time we truly need our homes is when it rains. Other than that we just enjoy nature.

My favorite fruits are apples and pomegranates, but we have all kinds. We have berries, too. Vegetables grow wild all over Eden. We have potatoes and turnips and tomatoes and carrots. There are also lots of beautiful flowers everywhere, of every different kind, shape and fragrance.

The best thing about Eden though, for a young man of eighteen like me, is the girls. They are beautiful, and they are everywhere. To me, the beauty of a flower or the taste of an orange can never compare with a girl of sixteen or seventeen, walking naked through the leaves, just waiting to make love to me. And the girls love to make love. Maybe not as much as a guy like me, but almost. And that's the best part. There's always love to go around. A well-endowed man, or even a not so well endowed, can never go lacking. It's usually a different girl every night, but if I love one I can keep her for longer. Girls usually like to stick with me; they don't get tired of me easily. I have the moves to keep them interested long after the first encounter. But there are no rules, no expectations. Just love, with no attachments.

Get a girl pregnant, of course, and it's a little bit of a headache. It's common decency to stay with a girl for a year or so after she gives birth, to help her out with the baby. Life is a lot less fun if that happens, and if the girl has male relatives, they can get pretty upset if you don't do your duty. But luckily the girls in Eden don't get pregnant all that often. There are some herbs they eat that keep them infertile. So that love can, you know, be had only for the sake of love, without the headache of children coming along the way.

I said that everyone's pretty much equal in Eden. That's true, although there's one man that everyone looks up to. His name is Adam, and he lives by himself, apart from the others. The only person that is always by his side is a woman, Eve. People who've seen her say she's the most beautiful woman in all the world. Adam is the only man I've heard of who has kept only a single girl for himself all his life. Maybe it's just that there's no one to compare with the girl he already has, Eve. But people say that they've made some sort of agreement or pact, to be together forever. Just the two of them. It has a nice ring to it, a little romantic if you ask me. It sounds like something I say to the prettiest girls when I'm about to make love to them for the first time. But to actually do that is crazy. The commitment, the dedication it entails. That's just not the kind of life we live in Eden.

People say that Adam and Eve are kind, though. People go to them with their problems, sometimes traveling from far away to receive their encouragement and advice. I heard a man say once that Adam is like a shelter on a stormy day; he shields you from the difficulties of life if you go to him for help. People consider him a kind of holy man. There's this aura of awe and reverence about him that people respect and bow to. He'd be the closest thing to a leader that Eden had, if Eden had leaders. I've never visited Adam, though. Hearing stories about him is enough to satisfy my interest; I figure I can let the man live in peace. Besides, I don't have any problems to speak of.

I just realized that I haven't introduced myself yet. My name is Emmanuel. Like I said, I'm eighteen and loving life. I don't know who my parents are. Some people just don't. I've been on my own since as long as I can remember. But as they say, it takes a village. And ever since I've come of age, I've had plenty of female companionship to keep me company. So I've never been lonely. The girls say I'm good-looking. That's why all the pretty ones choose me first. I have to admit, I can be pretty charming to the ladies. It's hard not to be when you've got no cares and you have everything you'll ever need all around you. Yeah, the girls love me.

I went out hunting a deer this morning. I woke up before the woman I've slept with the past two nights; I left her sleeping in the tall grass underneath a canopy of trees shading her from the morning's light. I took my wooden spear with me. There are plenty of deer in the meadows of Eden, it didn't take me too long to find one. It looked at me curiously from behind its long nose as I slowly walked up to it. Then I thrust my spear into its belly and it fell on its knees, just like that. It looked saddened, shocked by what I had done, but I quickly removed my spear and thrust it into its heart. It was a bit messier than I would have liked; a good, clean kill extinguishes the life of the deer instantly, preserving it from sorrow and pain. But that is life here in Eden. Everything is for the good of us humans. The creatures here live to serve us, and we accept their services and sacrifices gratefully.

I picked the deer up by the legs and slung it across my shoulders, and carried it the short distance back to my tent. There I used a knife carved out of a sharpened rock to skin the animal and cut strips of meat from its bones. Then I gathered wood and made a fire, and cooked the meat I had prepared. This process took me into the early afternoon. The smoky smell of the cooked meat, which made a delicious barbeque, filled the air and must have traveled some distance because soon it attracted a sight that brought joy to my eyes. A beautiful girl, Adira, whom I hadn't seen for months, or maybe a year, suddenly appeared as I was taking the meat off the fire. She was wearing a deerskin gown the color of her own tanned skin, that made me wonder what she looked like beneath. Her bare feet danced merrily along the grass as she ambled toward me, her light brown hair flowing behind her pretty shoulders, her green eyes laughing as she saw the effect she had on me. I was taken from the moment I saw her.

I stared mischievously into her eyes as she approached and gave her an easy smile. "You must be hungry," I said, "because you've come to my tent just in time for lunch."
"I could smell the food as I was walking nearby, and I came to see what the occasion was," she said. "I have to admit, I haven't eaten yet. Can I join you?"

"There's more than enough for both of us," I said. "You can sit down with me. But I hope you won't leave too soon after you're done."

"We'll see how good your cooking is, Emmanuel," she said, smiling happily.

"You must have liked my cooking last time you were here, or you wouldn't have remembered my name," I told her.

"You gave me more to remember than just your cooking," the girl said. "And do you remember my name?"

"Adira, of course," I said. "I wouldn't forget a girl as beautiful as you. If I recall, we spent four or five nights together. You didn't want to leave."

"You wouldn't let me leave, silly boy," she said. "Now can we eat?"
I gave her a wooden plate with some deer meat on it, and served myself as well.

"Not bad," she said thoughtfully as she chewed. "It could use some vegetables on the side, though."

"Cooking multiple dishes is for the women to do," I said. "I just felt like deer today."

"Vegetables are good for you, you know."

"Or so the old women say. I think that's just a myth. I'm kind of glad I never knew my mother, or she would have filled my head with all kinds of worthless thoughts like that."

"It's not worthless to prolong your life," Adira said.

"We die when we die," I said. "It's how we enjoy ourselves while we live that matters."

She leaned over her plate and kissed me full on the mouth. "Did you enjoy that, silly boy?" she asked.

"Too much," I said. "Now I want more, and I won't let you leave me even if you want to."

"It's lucky that I don't want to leave, then," Adira said. "Tell me, what did you enjoy more, my lips or the deer you burnt?"

"I didn't burn the deer," I said, "but of course your lips tasted better."

"Come drink your fill, then," she said. I put my meat down and leaned over to kiss her again, but she got up and danced away, giggling.

"If you want me to chase after you, you should take your gown off to give me a better view of who I'm after," I called. But she just ran, and I got up and ran after her.

Adira was slender and shapely, and I thought of the beauty I would have all to myself in just a moment. I chased her into a grove of apple trees, and then I couldn't see her any more.

"Adira?" I asked, as I walked through the grove. "Adira?" I picked up a ripe apple from the ground and bit into it as I searched for her. Suddenly I felt two slender arms around my waist. Adira had grabbed me from behind, and she pushed me to the ground, falling on top of me laughing. I rolled over and let her rest her head on my chest.

"You're so strong," she said, lazily. "Where did you get all these muscles?"

"Did you know I'm the best wrestler out of all of my friends, too?" I boasted.

"Let me see," Adira said. She took my shirt off and put her hands on my chest. "Very handsome. I approve."

"Are you the only one that gets to appreciate the beauty of nature today?" I asked her from my back. She was sitting on top of me now.

"No," she said. "Nature is for both of us to enjoy." She brought the top of her gown down from over her breasts to her waist. She was a sight to behold. Her breasts were plump and firm, and her belly button twinkled on her smooth belly.

"You're beautiful," I said, pulling her down on top of me. We made sweet love for hours among the sweet fallen apples beneath the trees in the apple grove. I don't know exactly how long. All I know is that eventually, satisfied from long love, I fell asleep with my face in her breasts, and she fell asleep beneath me. When I woke up the stars were out, the night was a little cool, and she was gone.

"The little nymph," I said to the fireflies. "I could have spent five nights with her again."

I was hungry. I hadn't eaten much lunch. I walked back to my home in the shining moonlight, and found a woman sitting in front of my tent, eating the rest of Adira's deer.

"Shiphrah?" I asked. "You're back."

"I decided I wanted you for one more night," the woman said. She let her gown slip down past one shoulder, exposing her left breast.

"And I didn't think you wanted to be alone."

"Why did you think I would be alone?" I asked.

"I know things," Shiphrah said. "I saw your lunch here half-eaten today. You must be hungry."

I sat down to the plate I had left before, across from Shiphrah. I reached over and pulled her gown back over her shoulder.

"I've had my fill of love today," I said. "But I would have you keep me company tonight."

"No one likes to sleep alone," Shiphrah said, chewing on her meat. The woman was older than me, nearly thirty. Still, she had large green eyes, a dazzling smile, and a shapely body. I enjoyed her company.

As we ate, Shiphrah told me of the man she had met when she had left my tent the day before. He was young and good-looking, she said, and she had wanted to spend the night with him, but then a younger girl had come along and the man had chosen her instead. I saw the pain the rejection had caused in her eyes.

"But there are plenty of willing young men in Eden," I said, "and you're still beautiful." I softened in my attitude toward her, and the slightly injured creature suddenly seemed more attractive to me.

"And I think that I'm still in the mood for love after all."
We went into my tent. There were flowers scattered around the floor. It must have been Shiphrah.
"Thank you, Emmanuel," she said to me as I removed her gown.
"I must warn you, I've already had my share of sleep," I said.
"I'm not tired," she said to me, with a love-starved gaze.
 She made love to me vigorously that night.

2

And they were both naked, the man and his wife, and they were not ashamed.

Genesis 2:25

I woke up shortly before dawn with Shiphrah sleeping in my arms. Her face was snuggled against my chest and her long auburn hair lay scattered across my shoulders. She had both arms around my waist and, in her sleep, she was clenching me tight. I had one arm wrapped around her and with the other I softly rubbed her fragile hands.

I was saddened by how much the man's rejection from the night before had hurt her. She was a beautiful woman, one of the most beautiful I knew, but she feared the day when age would rob her of her most prized possession. A woman who lost her sexual attractiveness lived alone, unwanted by the young men at night, and Shiphrah feared that. I wished that I could somehow reassure her that she still had time—ten years at least before she lost her allure—but I knew that the best I could do was love her now.

As a man I had less to fear—there would always be a woman to sleep with me until I lost my vigor, and after that I would have no desire for women anyway. I wouldn't mind being alone. I was a strong man and I could fend for myself.

Shiphrah smelled like flowers. I kissed the top of her head. I didn't want her to be afraid.

After a few minutes I gently escaped Shiphrah's grasp and got out of bed. She stirred but didn't awake. I thought she was dreaming. I went outside and looked at the first streaks of light over the trees on the horizon. The sky was rolling with clouds flooded with red, orange, yellow and pink. Behind me the sky was still dark blue, and I could see a few bright stars lingering in the sky. The sun wasn't out yet.

I looked at the deer meat I had cooked yesterday. I didn't feel like meat this morning. I thought I would go pick some potatoes and berries and prepare breakfast before Shiphrah woke up. I walked out into the misty morning. There was a light dew on the grass and the crickets were still chirping. The birds were also out, and they flew and sang happily as I walked beneath them.

The sound of footsteps came to me from behind the tall grasses I was plodding through. I wondered if it was an animal. I hadn't brought a spear with me. If it was a bear I would have to scare it off. I looked around for a rock. I found one on the ground, and picked it up. The sound came closer. I stood ready and held the rock up in front of me. If I hit the bear hard enough, it would grow weary and leave me alone.

It wasn't a bear, however. It was a man. I vaguely recognized him from somewhere, but I couldn't remember his name.

"Put your rock down, Emmanuel. I am not here to hurt you." The man's voice was deep and rung out into the awakening morning.

"I do not remember your name," I replied curtly.

The man laughed. "But I remember yours. My name is Morag."

I casually tossed the rock back onto the grass. Then I approached the man and patted him on the shoulder. "How do I know you?"

The man turned serious. Small lines wrinkled around his eyes. "We met briefly some years ago. Simply crossed paths. But I believe you know my sister better."

"Your sister?" I asked uninterestedly. "And who would that be?"

"Sarah," the man replied, staring at me fixedly. "You know her quite well."

"Sarah, the girl with the tight thighs and pretty eyes?" I asked, with a flash of recognition.

"You would know," the man replied curtly.

I laughed. "Yes I would, Morag. As I recall, I spent quite some time with your sister some months ago. I liked her so much I told her I would never leave her. It made for a good fantasy at night."

Morag looked grim. "It made for more than a fantasy," he said.

I thought that Shiphrah would be waking up soon. "Look, Morag, I'm not sure what you're getting at, but I'm searching for breakfast. I have a woman who needs care this morning. Maybe you can come with me and we can talk while the potatoes cook.

"I've come a long way," Morag said. "I've walked a day and a half just to find you."

I smiled. "You must be hungry then," I said.

"My hunger can wait," the man said. He was getting impatient.

"What cannot wait is your duty to Sarah."

"My duty?" I said. "I have no bond to the girl."

"She's pregnant," the man said gruffly.

I laughed. "So that's what this is about. And I assume you think I'm the father. That's why you're here."

"I don't think, I know," Morag said.

"And how would you know that?" I asked. "How many men has Sarah been with this year? Why would you think it was me?"

"I saw it in a dream," Morag said.

I sighed. "We all dream, Morag. I don't see why you would think yours would somehow reveal the identity of the father of your sister's child. And I certainly don't hope that you think I am going to stay with the girl for a whole year just because you thought of me in your sleep."

"It isn't that easy," Morag said. "Sarah is frightened, because no one has come forward to accept responsibility for her. She doesn't want to raise the child alone. I know you're the father, Emmanuel. It's your duty to protect the girl."

"I don't believe it is," I said, looking around me. "Now, if you won't come with me, I will go looking for potatoes alone."

"We don't have many duties in Eden," Morag said. "But providing for the mother of your child is one of them. I won't let you go."
"And what will you do, stab me? I won't do any good to your little sister then. Besides, I'm bigger than you, Morag, You had best leave the matter alone."

"I will not."

I started walking again. "I'm going to find some potatoes."

Morag followed me. I let him. I walked for about five minutes, until I came across a few wild potatoes growing in a field near some blackberries. I dug out the potatoes and picked about thirty berries, placing them in a sheep-stomach bag I had brought with me.

"I have a woman waiting for me," I said. "You can come with us to have breakfast if you wish, before you head back to where you came from."

The man remained silent, but continued to follow me back to my tent. Then he said, "This woman you are with, let us see what she has to say about my dream."

"I doubt anybody would take this dream of yours too seriously," I said. "But sure, I'll humor you."

The sun was out now and felt warm on my skin. It would be a hot day. I returned to my camp to find Shiphrah seated outside my tent. She got up when she saw me and beamed me a smile.

"I see you brought breakfast, Emmanuel, and a friend."

"This is Morag," I said, taking the potatoes out of the bag and placing them over the fire. "He seems to think that I am the father of his sister's child."

Shiphrah looked at me. "If a man agrees he is the father, he is bound by duty to a woman and child for one year. Do you agree you're the father, Emmanuel?"

"I don't," I replied. "And Morag has no proof."

"I saw it in a dream," Morag replied angrily. "Tell this man that what I saw was the truth."

Shiphrah turned serious. "It is unusual for a man to dream about the father of his sister's child," she said. "If Morag claims it, he might be telling the truth."

"I don't doubt that he dreamt it," I said, "But I doubt that his dream meant anything."

"That's what I mean," Shiphrah said. "You should take this seriously."

I felt annoyed. "He came here just to hear you say that," I told her. "You're encouraging him. I was hoping he'd leave after breakfast."

"I cannot leave until you swear to look after my sister," Morag said.

"It's not often you see a man know who his sisters are, much less take care of them," Shiphrah said. "I admire you, Morag."

Morag looked satisfied with himself. I sighed.

"Morag is wasting his time here," I said. "I have no interest in providing for Sarah."

"You should think this through carefully," Morag said. "Sarah has more male relatives who won't be happy with your decision."

"So there's a whole clan of you," I said. "Are you threatening me?"

"We look after each other," Morag said. "And if you're not useful to Sarah, you're not useful at all. That is absolutely a threat."

I stood up. "I think it's time for you to leave," I said. "You can find breakfast on your way home."

"Emmanuel, are you sure that's wise?" Shiphrah asked. But Morag had stood up too. "He's made his choice," he said darkly. Then he fixed me with a stare full of hatred. "But you'll pay for it, coward."

I laughed. He looked much too serious. "Good riddance, fool," I said. Morag stalked angrily off.

Shiphrah sighed. "He's going to come back for you, Emmanuel," she said quietly.

"Let him. I'm twice as strong as he is."

She put her hand on one of my muscular arms. "I don't doubt that. But people have been killed over matters like this before."

"Let him come," I repeated.

I turned my thoughts to the potatoes. I turned them over the fire. They cooked for a few more minutes, and then I took them off. I gave one to Shiphrah. "I brought blackberries too," I said.

We ate in silence for a while. Then Shiphrah put her plate down and kissed me. "I don't want you to get hurt," she said. "You cared for me last night when I needed someone. Let me stay with you for a few days, at least until I'm sure Morag and his relatives aren't coming back."

"You're a good lover," I said. "You can stay."

Shiphrah smiled, and ran her hand through my long black hair. "Did I ever tell you how handsome and noble you look with your hair flowing over your shoulders?" she said. "I like you, Emmanuel."

"Come sit on my lap," I said. The woman crawled onto my thighs. I was much bigger than she was, and I felt like I was holding a child.

"You have a lot of years left in you. Did you know that?"

"I fear the future, Emmanuel."

"Don't. Everything will be okay."

We made love again outside the tent, beneath the beating sun. Shiphrah was savage with me, which I found pleasurable. At one point I was so lost in her embrace that we almost rolled into the fire. Afterward we got up and went to find dinner. I took a spear and went hunting, and Shiphrah wandered off to find vegetables. I killed a few rodents and brought them back to roast over the fire. Shiphrah was already back.

"Did you make love to me like that because you're afraid I'll make you leave?" I asked Shiphrah.

She just smiled at me under her eyelashes. "I like you, Emmanuel."

As she promised, she stayed with me for a few more days. On the third night, I was laying in my tent with Shiphrah in my arms when I heard a sound outside. I thought it was probably just an animal, but I remembered Morag's threat and I went outside my tent to make sure.

The night was still and quiet. I didn't see anything in the dim firelight, but I threw some brush on the fire and it flared upwards. Then in the distance I thought I saw a shadow move.

"Who's there?" I said. Just as I said it, I saw something flying at me out of the corner of my eye. A spear. I ducked and it flew over my head. Then I saw two of them jumping out of the bushes. I heard more footsteps behind me. A jabbing pain sliced through my left shoulder. Someone had thrust a spear into me from behind.

Bad move. Blood had been drawn, and I had no reservations about responding in kind. I would worry about the injury later. I grabbed the spear and pulled it out of my shoulder. Blood gushed from the wound, but I turned around and thrust the spear into the stomach of my assailant. He gasped in pain and surprise and yelled out to his friends. I pushed him backward a few steps and then drove him into the ground. Then I pulled the spear out and was about to thrust it into his heart when pain shot through the back of my skull.

Someone had struck me on the head with a rock. I fell over the man I had attacked, dazed. I couldn't see clearly, and I struggled to get up. Then I saw the shape of the rock descend toward my face again in a blur. I raised my left hand and grabbed it before it hit me. Then another man tackled me from the side.

We fell together in a heap onto the grassy ground, but as I fell I wrenched the rock from the second man's hand. My head and shoulder were hurting, but I struck at the man who had tackled me with all my might. I hit him twice on the head as another man jumped on top of me, knocking the rock from my hand. We wrestled together and the man who had struck me with the rock joined the fight. He kicked me in the side and then in the face. Blood flowed from my nose.

One man held me on the ground and the other man held up another rock in his hand. He looked like he was about to strike me but then a look of shock and terror registered in his eyes. The tip of a spear was protruding out of his stomach. Shiphrah had struck him from behind. I elbowed the man who was holding me and broke from his grasp. I got up before he did and punched the man Shiphrah had stabbed in the face. When he fell, I pulled the spear out of his back and faced the last man. I pointed it at him as he got up.

"Emannuel," the gruff voice said.

"Morag?" I said. "I told you I was too strong for you."

"If the woman hadn't helped you you'd be dead," the man said.

"Sarah and I have more relatives and friends. They won't be happy with what you've done tonight."

"You all should learn to leave well enough alone," I said. But Morag grabbed the rock I had dropped and threw it at me with all of his might. It hit me in the chest and a terrible pain shot through two of my ribs. But when he got up to rush me, I ran him through with the spear. Blood spilled out of his mouth as I drove him backwards. I pulled the spear out and stabbed him through the collarbone. He fell to his knees, stunned. I kicked him over onto his back.

Then I went to check on the other men. They were dead, except for the man I had stabbed in the stomach. He was moaning in a pool of blood. I kicked him in the face, and he fell onto his back.

"He'll be dead soon," Shiphrah said, standing beside me.

I smiled weakly at her, but then I collapsed onto the ground.

Shiphrah knelt down beside me, concerned. "You've lost a lot of blood," she said. "Let me help you into the tent.

With a great deal of effort, I got up and walked with Shiphrah's help into the tent. Shiphrah took some beaver skin and wrapped my shoulder with it. "I am going to heat a rock to cauterize your wound," she said. "I'll be back in a few minutes."

My head was hurting terribly, and as I lay there waiting for her my eyes started to blur again. Then everything became cloudy, and I drifted off into darkness.

3

Then the Lord God took the man and put him in the garden of Eden to tend and keep it.

And the Lord God commanded the man, saying, "Of every tree of the garden you may freely eat; but of the tree of the knowledge of good and evil you shall not eat, for in the day that you eat of it you shall surely die."

Genesis 2:15-17

I don't know how long it was before I awoke, but Shiphrah was there, sitting over me. Locks of her hair flowed over her face and onto my cheek, and there were tears in her blue eyes. She brought a cup of water to my lips. I drank.

"Shiphrah…"

"Shhh…" she said. "Quiet. Don't speak."

The terrible pain in my head was considerably lessened, but I saw that Shiphrah had wrapped my head in bandages she had made out of deerskin. The wound on my shoulder burned, but the bleeding had stopped.

I tried to get up, and my ribs caught fire. A couple of them might have been broken.

"Stay still," Shiphrah said, giving me some more water. "You're hurt. I've made some food. Don't get up."

Shiphrah left the tent, and returned a few seconds later with cooked carrots and corn. She fed them to me as I lay on my back. After I ate, I thanked her.

"You didn't have to do this," I said. "Has anyone else arrived since I blacked out?"

"No one," Shiphrah said.

We talked for a while about what had happened.

"Morag has friends," I told Shiphrah. "I am afraid some of them might come back here to avenge him. It's not safe here for you. I want you to leave."

"I can't do that," Shiphrah said. "You need someone to care for you."

"I'll be fine," I said.

I tried to sit up again, but gave up the effort. Shiphrah smiled at me compassionately.

"You're a strong man," she said. "You took all of them on by yourself."

"I needed the help of a woman," I said.

"That's not so shameful. You need women for other things too."
It started to rain outside. The patter of raindrops sounded on the walls of the tent.

"I guess you're stuck here with me for a while," I said to Shiphrah. I reached up my hand and caressed her cheek.

She held my hand in hers. "You'll be okay."

We sat there in silence, with only the splash of rain on the tent and ground outside audible. I looked at Shiphrah. I was hurt, but I wanted her, maybe more so because of my injury.

"Shiphrah," I said softly.

She turned to look at me brightly. "Yes?"

"Make love to me."

"In your condition?"

"Make me forget Morag and his friends. Make me forget my pain."

"They say love is more pleasurable with pain," Shiphrah said.

Slowly Shiphrah removed my loincloth, and sat on top of me. She made love to me sitting, as I lay there on my back. I grimaced in pain, but soon closed my eyes and lost myself in the sensation.

"You haven't lost your beauty, Shiphrah," I finally said.
Shiphrah had put her clothes back on when there was noise outside the tent. Someone was opening it.

"You should have gone," I said in a low voice. "I can't defend you like this."

But it wasn't one of Morag's friends that had come for me. It was his sister.

"Sarah?" I asked.

Shiphrah looked annoyed. "What do you want with him?" she said.

But there were tears in Sarah's eyes. She was shorter than Shiphrah, and more slender, with long black hair and black eyes. Despite her sadness, she had a radiant face and attractive figure.

"I saw my brothers and uncle outside," Sarah said. "Is it true that you killed them?"

"I killed them," I replied, "but only because they attacked me."

"I think Morag was right. You are the father of my child."

"Because we spent a few nights together? I have no interest in you or your child."

"I thought you'd say that," Sarah said. "Still, I have come to warn you. Morag has more brothers and they all have friends. They knew about what you've done to him. They will want revenge. Because you're the father of my child, I didn't want you to die."

"So you've come to warn me? After what I've done?"

"You're irresponsible, Emannuel, but you're a good man. I know your heart."

I closed my eyes. "There will be others to care for you and your child," I said. "You should go now. It's dangerous here."

Sarah walked over to me and kissed me on the forehead. "I'm sorry about what happened to you," she said. And then she disappeared into the rain.

"Strange girl," Shiphrah said. But Sarah's unexpected warmth had felt good.

"You should go too, Shiphrah. You've done enough for me."

"You'll die alone," Shiphrah said.

"I have friends," I said. "They will fight for me. Go to Heber and Ebron. Tell them what's happened. They'll know what to do."

"I hope you make it through this, Emannuel," Shiphrah said. "Do you need anything else?"

"Not right now," I said. "Go." Shiphrah left.

I lay there for hours. Then I determined to sit up. Ignoring the pain, I lifted myself off the ground. My ribs burned, but they would heal. I took a drink of water, then I thought that if I was sitting up I might as well stand up and walk around.

I got up onto my feet. The rain had stopped. I went outside. I found a spear lying around where the battle had been, and I picked it up. I felt it in my hands. I had a broken rib or two, but I could fight if necessary.

The bodies of Morag and his relatives were gone. Shiphrah must have dragged them off into the forest before she left.

There was still enough deer meat and vegetables to last me for several days, and I had nothing else to do so I went back into the tent. My head was aching again. I lay back down on my blankets and went to sleep.

I awoke to the sound of laughter. Heber and Ebron, my two best friends, were standing in my tent and joking at my condition.

"He looks like a bear mauled him," Ebron said.

"I don't think so. I think the women were probably just too rough with him last night."

They both laughed again.

"Very funny," I said. "You'll both look like me soon enough."

Heber looked at me with a gleam in his eye.
"Meyer, Caleb and Ram are outside. We have more friends coming."
I smiled. "Morag was an old fool, and his friends will be too if they come for us."

"That they will, Emmanuel," Ebron said. "Morag's uncles have gathered a crowd about them. Fifteen, maybe twenty men. They are going to attack in a few days."

"What do their friends have against me?" I asked.

Heber shrugged. "Fighting is fun. Ebron and I are having the time of our lives already."

The two men laughed again. I sat up despite the pain.

"We'll need spears, clubs and rocks," I said.

"We have spears and clubs with us," Ebron said.

"I'll help you gather rocks," I said.

"We'll take care of that," Heber said, putting his hand on my shoulder. "You need to rest and regain your strength. We'll need our best wrestler healthy for the fight that is coming."

"It's good of you to fight for me," I said.
"That's what friends are for," Ebron said. "Now if only we could be as faithful to women."

"If only women could be as faithful to us," Heber said.

The two young men laughed again. I chuckled despite the pain.

"You know," Ebron said, "It wouldn't have been so bad to have Sarah to yourself for a year. She's a pretty girl."

"You know I don't do things like that unless I have to," I said. "I like my freedom."

"We all do," Ebron agreed.

"That's what we're fighting for, then," Heber said. "Freedom!"

"A noble cause, Emmanuel," Ebron said.

"You two would do anything for a thrill," I said. "You might die from this, you know."

"We all live for but a time," Heber replied, "and when we die, we die."

"It's all about how good our women are while we live," Ebron said.

"And you know how they make love to men who are back victorious from a fight," Heber said.

We all laughed, mine with a grimace.

Meyer stuck his head inside the tent.

"Hi there, Emmanuel. Quite a bind you've gotten yourself into," he said. Then he turned to Ebron and Heber. "Caleb and Ram killed an ox. They say they need it to feed all the people who will be here. They need your help dragging it to the camp."

I got up to my feet. "Not you, Emmanuel," Ebron said. "We'll be back in an hour or so."

My friends left the tent. I lay down again.

That night, the smell of roast oxen filled the tent, and the sounds of laughter and merrymaking rose around it. More friends had come. I sat up with less difficulty. My ribs were healing quickly. I got up and went outside.

A great cheer went up from about fifteen young men who were gathered around the fire. "Emmanuel, the man of the hour! You're just in time for the oxen!"

I smiled. My injuries were healing, and I had friends around me.

"You all look like you're about to have a fight," I said.

"A man needs two things in life," Caleb said, "A woman every night, and a good man to fight."

"That's more than two things," Ram said. Everyone laughed.

Ebron looked up at me. "You look better," he said.

"I won't be young forever," I said. "I'll enjoy it while it lasts."

Some of the young men had brought spices and salt with them for the occasion, and the oxen was delicious. We enjoyed each other's company that night, and in the several days that followed. We had so much fun in our reunion that we almost forgot about Morag's friends who were coming. And I was feeling so much better I forgot I had been injured.

On the third day after Heber and Ebron had first come into my tent, one of our friends who had been keeping watch around our camp ran back breathlessly to report that twenty men were coming, armed with clubs and spears. Everyone ran for their weapons.

"Remember the strategy we discussed," I reminded them. "When they first come, throw your rocks at them. Then pick up your clubs and spears and fight alongside each other."

A few minutes later, the sound of angry shouts came from the forest. I held my rock firmly in my hand and stood calmly ready as my friends stood in a line beside me. I took a deep breath, and when the first man appeared out of the forest, I flung my rock at him with all my strength. It hit him squarely on the head and he fell to the ground, blood spilling everywhere. Then more men appeared. The others threw their rocks at them as I picked up my spear. Several more men fell down, injured and dead. Then the men were upon us. I pointed my spear at the man coming directly at me and ran him through the stomach. His eyes bulged outward as he gasped for air and collided with me, my spear sticking out of his back. I raised my club and hit him on the head. As he fell to the ground, he took my spear with him, and I raised my club, looking for the next man to attack.

The people around me had fallen into a melee. My friends had broken their line, and there was only a large crowd fighting in chaos. I picked a man and hit him in the back with my club with all of my might. There was a loud crack as wood crushed bones in his ribs and spine. The man spun around and lunged at me with his spear as he fell. I stepped to the side but was horrified to see Ebron behind me receive the spear to his thigh.

I hit the man on the forehead with my club, which made a sickening crunch as it crushed his skull. Then I pulled the spear out of Ebron's thigh. Men were falling everywhere, and the ground was covered in blood. I spun around and saw another man coming at me with a rock. I lunged my spear at him and missed, and I ducked to avoid a blow from his rock. Then I tackled him to the ground. He thrashed at me with his arms as I punched him again and again in the face. Finally I took the rock from his hand and finished him off. There was blood all over my face, chest and arms, and its taste filled my mouth. The savagery was over in a few minutes. I got up and looked around. Caleb, Heber and four more of my friends were standing. Everyone else, including Ebron, was dead.

I walked over to where I had seen him last. His skull had been crushed from behind with a club. I knelt down beside his bloody remains and wept for the man. He was my friend.

Heber came up to me and put his hand on my shoulder. He gazed on Ebron sadly. "We won the fight," he said softly.

I buried my face in my hands and continued weeping. I couldn't stop. All of my friends had died for my sake.

Soon Caleb came up to us and said, "It's time to go. This place is a graveyard."

I took a deep breath and got up. "We can leave everything. I won't be coming back here."

Except for minor cuts and bruises, the seven of us left standing weren't injured.

"Let's go find some women," Heber said.

We all agreed. You can always count on a woman to make you forget your problems in Eden.

4

"And the Lord God said, "It is not good that man should be alone; I will make him a helper comparable to him."

Genesis 2:18

We trudged warily through the tall grasses and frequent trees, blood from the men we had killed trailing on the brush as we passed it. After about fifteen minutes I got tired of walking under the beating sun. I saw an orange tree and sat under its shade, picking an orange as I sat. As I began to peel the orange, Heber noticed that I had stopped walking and he told the rest of my friends to stop as well.

"What are you doing?" Heber said.

"The fight's over," I said. "Let me grieve for my friends."

"More of them could still be out there," Heber said.

"You don't really believe that," I said. "You just don't want to deal with the fact that Ebron is dead."

"Ebron died, as will you and I one day," Heber said. "That's just a fact. There's nothing else to deal with."

"I'm done walking."

Caleb stood beside Heber. "Let us not disband so quickly. We will rest here for a few minutes, and then we will go to the river to wash ourselves."

I ate a piece of my orange.

"Would any of you like some?" I asked. I held up a blood-stained slice of orange.

"I'm fine, thanks," Caleb said.

Heber sat down beside me. "You know, that was a hell of fight," he said. "All in all, I think we did pretty well."

"What were we thinking?" I asked. "That no one was going to die? It was foolish."

"Eden is a land of fools," Caleb said, grabbing an orange of his own and leaning against the tree.

We ate in silence. A few minutes later I stood up, picked another orange, and threw it as far as I could. Then I screamed into the fragrant air.

The rest of the young men got up as well. "Let's go get you washed off, Emmanuel," Heber said to me gently.

About fifteen minutes later we came to the river. Several beautiful women were bathing naked in its waters. They looked up at us with radiant smiles.

"So it's happened, then," one of the women said. She was standing waist-deep in the water, her long black hair flowing over her breasts. Sarah.

"Your friends are all dead," I said to her. "As are many of mine."

"But you are still standing," Sarah said, a cute smile on her face. She walked out of the water toward me. "The father of my child."

"Women," Heber said, walking toward the river. "I get the blond one."

"I don't want you," the blond girl, the most beautiful of the group, said. "I want the one who killed the most men today."

"How do you know I didn't?" Heber said, bemused.

"He has the most blood on him," she said, looking at me. "Emmanuel, isn't it?"

"I believe we've met," I replied. "I should warn you, I do not feel gentle right now."

"I think I should have him," Sarah said. "After all, this war was fought for me."

The men were starting to walk into the water. I followed them in.

The blood had dried and hardened on my skin, and it wasn't coming off by itself. I scrubbed at my thighs weakly.

Heber walked up to the blond woman. "Let the two lovers have each other," he said. "I am the most wounded. Please try to comfort me."

The woman stared at him. "I haven't been with a wounded man for a long time," she said. "Will you let me lick your wounds?"

"It depends where your mouth has been," Heber replied.

The woman let out a startled laugh.

Caleb and the other men were scrubbing themselves vigorously. Sarah had come up to me and was pouring handfuls of water over my face and chest.

"Let me," she said.

She gently rubbed the sides of my face and arms with wet fingers.

The blood came gradually off.

"There," she said finally. "You look a little more like a man."

"Blood isn't your fantasy, then," I said.

She wrinkled her nose. "You're a good man, Emmanuel. Not a killer."

She was making me uncomfortable. "I'm not the father of your child, Sarah," I repeated. "Give it up."

Three of the men had gone off into the trees with the other women.

Then several men I vaguely knew walked toward the river. One of them glared at me. I glared back.

"Shelah," Sarah said. "Why are you here?"

"Why is he still standing?" the man growled.

"Emmanuel won the fight," Sarah said. "The men who fought for me are dead."

"Your brothers may have fought for you, but the others died to avenge them, a task apparently still unfinished."

"Don't make the same mistake they did," I said in a low voice.

Several more men had arrived to join Shelah, and they had spears.

"Caleb, go get Heber and the others," I said softly. Caleb got quickly out of the river and ran into the trees.

"Tell me why I shouldn't kill you now," Shelah said, taking one of the spears in his hand.

"Because there has been enough death today," a loud and authoritative voice said from the trees. Two men were standing there. One man was tall and muscular, with jet black hair and a brash smile in his eyes. The other was about half a head shorter, with brown hair braided to his waist, and a considerably graver look on his face.

Heber and the others arrived, the women beside them. "What is the meaning of this?" Heber said.

"There's going to be another fight, Heber," I said, getting out of the water.

"There will not," the tall newcomer said. "Adam has said it is enough."

"Adam?" Shelah asked. "Is he here?"

"No," the man said, "But I am his son, Cain. This is my brother Abel. Adam has sent us here to end the fight."

"Go ahead, Cain," I said. "Tell these men to let the matter rest, but I doubt they will listen to you."

"Adam has a message for you, Emmanuel," Abel said. He stared into my eyes, his gaze penetrating into my soul. "He knows who you are."

An uncomfortable feeling filled my breast as the young man spoke.

"How does Adam know me?" I asked. "And how do you know my name?"

"My father knows many things, Emmanuel," Abel said.

"Sarah's brother was right," Abel's older brother said. "My father says that you are the father of the child. He has ordered that you take responsibility for the mother until the child is born and has done nursing."

"Who is your father to give orders?" I demanded.

But Heber rebuked me. "Everybody in this land respects Adam, Emmanuel," my friend said. "If he says you are the father of the child, you must protect the girl."

"First a crazy dream, and now a man who doesn't even know me telling me what my duty is?" I said angrily.

"I won't fight for you if you ignore Adam's wisdom, Emmanuel," Caleb said. The other men murmured their assent.

"We will kill you if you do not apologize and accept the truth," Shelah said, his knuckles white around the spear.

"If you believe that what you say is true," I said to Cain, "then wrestle me, right here in front of everyone. If you win, I will watch after the girl. But if you lose, then you will tell my enemies to go back to their lives."

Cain studied me deeply. "I accept," he said.

Sarah stepped beside me and put her hand on my elbow. I turned to look at her. Her breasts were glimmering in the sunlight.

"Now is not the time for love, Sarah," I said.

"Emmanuel," she said sadly. "Do you really want to go through all of this trouble just to avoid me?"

"It's not about you," I said to her gently. "It's about me and the son of Adam now."

I hardly noticed Cain running at me until he was nearly on top of me. He tackled me to the ground.

"Woah," I said, shocked. "Don't hurt the girl just to get at me."
But Cain put both of his arms around my neck and started choking me. Surprised, I put one hand up against his face and with the other punched him several times in the side. He rolled off me, gasping for breath.

I jumped on top of him and knocked him onto his back. I pinned him to the ground with one hand and with the other made a fist. I struck at him with all my might, knocking out a bloody tooth.

Cain growled and kneed me in the groin. I doubled over in pain as he got up and kicked me in the side, and then in the face. I saw stars but I swung my leg around and tripped him to the ground. I took a moment to regain my bearings, but he was on top of me again, punching me in the face over and over again. I lifted a hand up and blocked one of his punches, and managed to say, "You fight like a woman."

Cain stopped punching me. He stared at me with wild rage. "And you will die like one," he said. Then he raised his hand over my head. He was holding a large rock.

"Cain!" Abel said. "Cain! Control your anger. Father does not want the man dead."

Cain hesitated, the rock shaking in his hand. Abel grabbed it from him, and pushed him back.

"Enough!" Abel said. "Our job is done here." Then he turned to me. "You have lost your wrestling match. You will care for the girl."

My mouth and nose were bleeding, and my groin hurt. I lay my head back down on the ground. Abel turned to the other men as Cain fumed behind him. "The rest of you are going to leave now. The matter with Sarah and Emmanuel is finished."

"And what of my friends who died because of him?" Shelah said.

"Will you oppose the will of Adam?" Cain said. He had cooled down a little.

Shelah studied him. "No." He turned to the other men. "Let's go."

Heber knelt down beside me. "You lost to a son of Adam," he said. "There's no shame in that."

"So the girl is my responsibility after all."

"I will leave you to her," Heber said. Caleb and my other friends also said their goodbyes, and disappeared back into the trees with the women. I was left alone with Sarah.

She took my hand and helped me to my feet. There was a grin on her face.

"Looks like you went through a lot of trouble to avoid this moment," she said.
"You must be mistaken," I said. "Why wouldn't I appreciate the prospect of domestic bliss with you?"

"Rearing a child with me won't be that bad, you'll see," Sarah said. "Lots of men enjoy a period of time alone with a woman."

I washed my bloodied face with a few handfuls of water. "At least you're attractive," I said.

"Is that all?" she said.

"No," I said. My nose wouldn't stop bleeding. I thought it was broken. "No, not at all. You're also very strange."

"And why is that?" Sarah asked merrily. She was apparently very pleased with herself.

"You know exactly why," I said.

"Because you killed my family and friends, and I still want you?" she said.

"That's a start," I said.

She smiled again. "I just have this feeling about you, Emmanuel. I think you and I are meant to be together."

"Until the child is weaned, I hope you mean," I replied warily.

"Maybe," she said evasively.

"I hope you don't think we have an Adam and Eve thing, Sarah," I said. "Just you and I, for the rest of our lives? I don't think so."

She remained quiet.

I sighed. "You're impossible!" I said.

"I didn't say anything," she said.
"I know, and I will gladly let you keep your thoughts to yourself."

"You look terrible, Emmanuel. Cain beat you up pretty bad."

"I told the man I wanted to wrestle, not fight to the death. There's something wrong with his head."

"I thought you were the best wrestler in Eden."

"He kneed me in the groin."

Sarah stood close against me, her nether parts rubbing against mine. "Speaking of, how is your groin feeling?"

"I don't feel like love right now, Sarah. I am still grieving for my friends."

Then I thought of something. I held her at arm's length, and looked down at her stomach. There was no bulge there.

"I thought they said you were pregnant," I said to her, alarmed. "I see no evidence of a child."

Sarah grabbed my hands and held them in hers. "Morag saw that I was pregnant in his dream," she said.

I snorted. "Morag and his dreams," I said. "You are all crazy."

Sarah laughed. "You need to believe more, Emmanuel."

"Believe in what?" I asked.

"In things. Good things, beautiful things. Things like dreams, and the wisdom of Adam."

"Where are your clothes, anyway?" I said to the naked girl. The clothes were lying on the other shore of the river, a deerskin shirt and gown. She waded through the water and picked them up. I watched her as she bent over to put them on. Very tight thighs indeed.

I sat down and covered my face in my hands. My head was swimming. Cain had punched me viciously. I laid my head down and closed my eyes.

Several minutes later, I felt a tugging on my loincloth. Sarah was unwrapping it.

I opened an eye. "What are you doing?" I asked. "I told you I'm not in the mood for love."

She threw the cloth to the side. "You're bruised," she said. Then she lowered her head. "I'll make you feel better."

I closed my eyes. The girl didn't take no for an answer.

5

Then the rib which the Lord God had taken from man He made into a woman, and He brought her to the man.

Genesis 2:22

Sarah and I wandered for a few days among the fruit trees and berry bushes, searching for a new place to live. My old home held no interest for me. We came across a deer on the way and stopped as I roasted it over a lazy fire. Sarah lounged around bored as I worked. I didn't look at her, absorbed in my cooking. Finally she spoke up.

"Why aren't you talking?" she asked.

I stared at the meat roasting on the fire. I had put wild spices on it, and its smell made my mouth water. "I don't have anything to say," I finally replied.

"That's not the Emmanuel I know," she said.

I turned to look at her. "Or maybe it's that you won't want to hear what I have to say."

"And what is that?" Sarah asked curiously. Her bright eyes beamed at me.

"Oh I don't know," I said, looking down again. "I don't want this. I don't want to be with you for a year. I don't even know if you're pregnant."

She walked up behind me and grabbed my hands, turning me toward her. "Look at me," she said. I looked into her hopeful eyes. "I don't believe you."

"Then what do you believe?" I asked her, looking down again. I turned away toward the meat.

"I believe that you're just upset that Morag was right. That your friend Ebron died for nothing."

I poked at the meat on the fire a little bit more harshly than I should have. It fell into the flames.

"Sorry," Sarah said. "I didn't mean it that way."

I sighed, stabbing at the meat. It was now covered in ash. "Ebron knew what he was getting into," I said. "They all did."

Sarah came closer to me and put her hands on my shoulders. "You said yesterday that I was beautiful," she said.

I managed to get the meat back onto its skewer. "I hope you don't mind the taste of soot."

Sarah didn't say anything.

I turned around to look at her. "You are beautiful," I said.

"Then why don't you want me?" she asked.

I took a deep breath. "You don't know me, Sarah," I said. "You think you do. You say I am a good man. I am good, but I'm not responsible. I don't know what it's like to care for a woman. I like to be free, to do what I want."

She gazed deeply into me with her black eyes. "You're young, Emmanuel. We both are. You'll grow. You'll learn."

I took the meat off the fire. "Do you feel like eating this?" I asked. The deer looked miserable.

"You made it," Sarah said. "And I'm hungry."

The next day we came to a clearing near a grove of fig trees. There were fields full of wild vegetables nearby, and a bright, clear stream flowed softly only a few minutes' walk away. Birds were chirping happily as they hopped from tree to tree, and a few white clouds floated lazily in an otherwise sunny sky.

"I think we can live here," I said. "Heber and a few other friends live nearby, too."

"I had friends near this place too, but now they're all dead," Sarah said sadly. She looked down at the ground.
"They tried to kill the father of your child," I replied.

Sarah looked up at me. "What did you say?" she asked.

I studied the back of my hand. "Despite what I said to Cain, I admire Adam, too. I believe him."

"Then why did you have to fight Cain?" Sarah asked.

I sighed. "You were right about Ebron," I replied. "I didn't want for him to have died for nothing."

Sarah didn't say anything, but skipped to the other side of the clearing. "We can build a hut here," she said.

"There should be oxen nearby," I said. "I will kill a few and use their skins for a roof."

Over the next few days I built our hut. When I killed the oxen, I found Heber and had him help me drag them back to the clearing. Sarah cooked the meat while I worked on the hut. She had a way with spices and vegetables.

I fashioned the walls of the hut with low-hanging branches I broke off of trees and strung the ox skins over them. It was large enough to fit the two of us, and a child, comfortably. Various people occasionally wandered by our new home, saying hello and complimenting me on my victory over Morag. They had all heard the story of what had happened with Adam's son, and they were glad to see me keeping my promise to Sarah.

One day I was out in the forest alone, gathering firewood, when a woman who was looking for berries appeared. I had never seen her before, and she was beautiful. More beautiful than Sarah.

She smiled at me. "Hello," she said.

I didn't say anything.

"Are you Emmanuel?" she asked.

"How do you know my name?" I asked.

"People talk about you, about what Adam told you to do. Take care of that girl, Sarah. I know people who died for her."

"So you do," I said. I went back to gathering firewood.

The young woman spoke again. "Don't you think I'm beautiful?" she asked.

"Are you trying to seduce me, the man whom Adam told must be faithful to another woman?"

She looked me up and down. She was. "It can get tiring, being with only one woman for so long. I know how you must feel."

I doubted her. "Have you ever been bound to a man?" I asked.

She smiled. "Yes. But I found ways to satisfy my desire."

I went back to gathering firewood. The woman spoke again. "I live nearby, if you're interested," she said.

I pretended I didn't hear her, and when I finally looked up, she was gone.

I walked slowly back to the hut, a stack of firewood in my arms, a little agitated. It was the first time a girl had come onto me since I had promised to protect Sarah. She was beautiful and seductive, and I felt tempted. I tried to sort through my feelings. Sarah left nothing to be desired. She was good company, and the sex was satisfying. I didn't know why my thoughts felt so confused.

My mind soon turned to another matter, however. When I got back to the clearing, I heard voices inside the hut. Sarah was speaking with another man.

"Sarah!" I called, as I dropped the firewood on a pile near the fire. "Who's in there with you?"

Sarah came out of the hut, a radiant smile on her face. "Emmanuel!" she said joyfully. "We have a special guest."

A man followed her gracefully out of the hut, and looked at me with a warm smile. "Emmanuel!" he said.

"Abel!" I said. "What business does a son of Adam have here?" His long hair fell to his waist, not in a braid this time, and his beard had been trimmed.

"I bring a message," he said. "But Sarah has made us lunch, and I am hungry. Let us eat first, and then we will talk."

We ate corn with black beans and spices, and beaver meat from the stream. Abel said that he was happy that I had kept my promise and stayed with Sarah.

"Adam will be very happy to hear of the home you have made," Abel said.

"It should last us until the child is weaned." I looked at Sarah. She smiled at me with her black eyes and dimples. Her stomach had grown larger, and now it was clear that she was with child.

"Tell me," Abel said. "How are you enjoying your time with the girl?"

"I have nothing to complain of," I said. "She has a joyful spirit, and she's good company."

"And you?" he turned to Sarah. "How is your time with Emmanuel?"

"He's a good man," she beamed. "And I think he's starting to like me more."

"I've always liked you," I said to Sarah.

She looked down. "So much that you fought for me," she said.

"I fought for my freedom," I said. "It had nothing to do with you."

"I know," Sarah said sadly.

Abel cleared his throat. "I think it's time I tell you what I came here to say."

"And what is that?" I asked.

Sarah gazed at Abel hopefully. Abel returned her gaze compassionately, and then looked at me seriously.

"Adam has had an inspiration about you," he announced. "He says that you must take this girl, Sarah, to wife."

"To wife?" I asked.

"It is what Adam himself has done with my mother, Eve," Abel replied firmly.

Sarah gasped, and covered her mouth with her hand. Understanding dawned on me as well.

"No," I said. "No, that wasn't part of the agreement."

Abel ignored me, and went on. "You must make a firm vow," he said, "to be with this girl for the rest of your life. You must love no one but her. You must be hers, and hers alone, forever."
Sarah had turned so radiant that her face shone with light, and her eyes were wet. "And I will be his," she gasped.

I got up from my seat and turned around. I started walking away.

"Where are you going, Emmanuel?" Abel asked.
I turned back around, and started pacing. I sat down again, and put my face in my hands.

"He's not taking this well, Abel," I could hear Sarah say.

"Get out." I said it so quietly that neither of them could understand me.

"What is it, Adam?" Sarah asked.

"Get out, Abel," I said louder, and looked up at him with eyes full of anger and impatience. Then I got up and screamed at him. "Get out!" Abel sat there firmly, and fixed me with a stare full of strength and dignity. He didn't move.

I started pacing again. "Who is Adam to tell me to do such a thing?" I muttered. "People listen to him. They will expect me to do as he says. Sarah has all sorts of ideas now. No one else has to do something like this. Why should I?"

Abel's voice rang out loud and clear, like a bell to my heart.

"You are capable of it, Emmanuel. Adam is expecting you."

I turned around. "What?" I asked.

"You are capable of it," Sarah said.

"I'll take care of this, Sarah," Abel said gently. "Adam is expecting you, Emmanuel."

"And why does he think I want to pay him a visit?" I asked.

"Because you are looking for answers," Abel said. He had gotten up too. Sarah got up with him.

I looked at them both incredulously.

"You and your father are insane," I said to Abel.
Abel hugged Sarah. "I must go now, precious," he said. Then he walked away, looking at me gravely as he passed. As he walked out of sight, he said loudly over his shoulder, "Follow the rising sun for two days. When you get to a fast-flowing river, follow the current for a day and a night. Adam will be waiting for you."

My head hurt. I walked past Sarah without looking at her, and into the hut. There I lay down and put my arm over my face. I couldn't think. Why was my life becoming so complicated?

Sarah gave me my space. She stayed outside until nightfall, and when she finally came in I felt a little clearer. I hated to admit it, but Abel was right. I was seeking answers, and Adam was the only one who could help me find them.

"Are you alright?" Sarah said to me gently. She had brought me a plate of food. I gently pushed it away.

"I don't know what's happening, Sarah," I said sadly. "I don't know what's happening to the world, what is happening to my life. Everything is changing."

"What's changing, Adam?" Sarah said softly. She sat down beside me and held my hands in hers.

I pulled my hands away. "My friends, my life, you. Adam and his sons." I didn't know how to explain it. I just felt uncomfortable with everything.

"Change isn't always bad," Sarah said. "Change can bring good things, too."

I turned away. "I want to go back to the way things were," I said. "I was happy before."

Sarah quietly started weeping. I looked at her. She was trying to stifle her sobs.

"Look, Sarah," I said. "I'm sorry."
Sarah kept weeping, and tears flowed down her lovely face.

"Come here," I said. She threw herself into my arms. I just held her as she sobbed onto my shoulder, until she became still.

"I will go see Adam," I said to her finally. But there was no response. Sarah had fallen asleep.

I gently lay her on the ground. I was restless. I had to go see Adam. I had to understand what this was all about. I needed answers.

I quietly left the hut and grabbed my spear. I ran through the trees for an hour, finally making it to Heber's house. He was asleep on the ground outside, with a girl in his arms. The girl from the forest.

"Heber," I said. "Heber."

Both he and the girl awoke. Heber raised his head tiredly. "Emmanuel?"

"I need you to do something for me," I said.

The girl wasn't happy about it, but Heber agreed to follow me into the forest. We killed an ox and dragged it back to my hut, where I skinned it and stripped the meat from its bones. Shortly before dawn, Sarah awoke.

"Heber? Emmanuel?" she asked, rubbing her eyes.

"Heber will care for you while I am gone," I said. "I've killed an ox and it should last you for awhile, but Heber will hunt more if you'd like."

"Are you going to see Adam?" she said. She seemed happy and content.

"Yes, Sarah. I will be traveling four days going there, and four days coming back. I don't know how long I'll be with Adam. Like I said, Heber has agreed to stay with you."
She smiled at me. She was fully awake now. "Oh, Emmanuel!" she ran up to me and wrapped her arms around my waist, burying her face in my chest. I patted her on the back.

"Sarah, I have to go. Abel said Adam is waiting for me."

"I know," Sarah said.

I shook Heber's hand. "Thank you," I said.

"Good luck, Emmanuel," Heber said.

"Emmanuel," Sarah said, as I walked off into the fig trees.

"Yes?" I asked.

"You're a good man."

6

And the Lord God formed man of the dust of the ground, and breathed into his nostrils the breath of life; and man became a living being.

Genesis 2:7

I was so confused. I wanted answers. I needed them. Why had Adam and his sons come into my life? I was doing fine on my own. I was content before. Why did Adam want me to marry Sarah? Why had he sent his sons to come visit me? I had wrestled with Seth, and he had almost killed me. He had only stopped because of Abel. Abel, who came and told me to stay with Sarah for the rest of my life. Just as his parents, Adam and Eve, had vowed to stay together.

It didn't make any sense. The question I kept asking was, why me? Why had Adam chosen to come to me with his message of fidelity? I didn't know if I could cross the will of so powerful a person. The respect he commanded among the people, his supernatural sagacity and wisdom, was too much to oppose. If Adam advised people to do something, people listened.

Then again, I might have been dead had Adam not intervened in my life anyway. Shelah and his friends could have killed me by the river. And if Cain and Abel hadn't come when they had, there might have been no end to the fighting and bloodshed. In Eden, such matters had a way of spiraling out of hand. It had happened before. Some said that my father had died in such a way, but I didn't know what role he had in the conflict, or if these rumors were even true. He was a father I had never known.

And what if Sarah's daughter was really mine? Would it have been reasonable for me to die fighting to avoid responsibility for a child I myself had conceived? Granted, establishing fatherhood in Eden was a formidable task. But Adam was never wrong. People knew that. And I knew it.

Why did Sarah want me so much? Why did she forgive me so freely, so effortlessly? It didn't make sense to me. A girl had never acted this way. It was so strange, so unnatural. And Adam supported her, wanted me to stay with her. He agreed with Sarah, I was sure of it. I wanted to know why.

When I got to the river Abel had spoken of, I saw a bear who was there hunting fish. It saw me and looked up. With it were three little cubs.

I didn't have a spear with me. I backed away slowly. It was knee-deep in water on the opposite shore of the river, which was maybe twenty feet wide. As Abel had said, its current was strong and rapid, but it didn't seem to be very deep. The bear could have easily crossed.

But the bear looked down at the river again, and threw its paw into the water. Then it cast its head in, and came up with a large fish. A salmon. Holding it with its teeth by the tail, the bear slapped the Salmon against the rocks, and then fed it to its cubs. I slowly walked on, ignored by the bear and its feeding children.

I ate the fruits, vegetables, and nuts growing wild all over Eden as I walked. There was always something to eat. As I drew closer to my destination, I began to get excited. So I was finally going to meet Adam, a man who knew me and thought enough of me to send his sons to intervene in my affairs.

I finally came to a young man who was standing by the stream, standing over a dead leopard. He had killed it with a spear tipped with a sharpened stone, which he was holding in his hand. I hadn't seen a leopard in years.

"My mother saw it this morning," he said. "Cain and Abel are gone on an errand, so I told my father that I would get it. I chased it around for hours, before it finally turned and fought."

"You must be Seth," I said.

"So you've heard of Adam's youngest son," the young man replied. He rinsed his bloody hand in the river and stood up majestically to shake mine. "And you are Emmanuel, of course."

"Abel told you I was coming?" I asked.

"I haven't seen my brother since he left home over a week ago," Seth replied. "My father told me."

"So Adam has his ways," I said.
Seth smiled. "He's expecting you. Go on ahead, we live only an hour away. I am going to skin this beast and bring the fur to my mother. She will make a garment or blanket out of it."

"I'll help you," I said.

"I'll be fine, Emmanuel," Seth said. "You came here to see my father, not to help me skin a leopard. Do not pause on account of me. I will see you again in the evening."

So I left him, and continued walking along the river. Eventually its current slowed and its waters became peaceful. Shortly afterward, I came to row upon row of vegetables, planted in an organized fashion. Orchards full of every kind of fruit stood off in the distance, farther away from the river. Beyond the vegetables, I saw three large huts covered in bear and beaver skins and then a cave beyond the entrance of which the river fell into a short waterfall. A fire was going outside one of the huts.

As I drew closer, I noticed a woman standing by the river, rinsing off a blanket. She was tall and beautiful, with light brown hair and blue eyes. Her face was so radiant that I blinked twice before clearing my throat and saying hello. A woman so stunning and elegant could only be Eve.

She smiled, stood up and held up a hand. Then she walked toward me, and when I was near enough, she said softly, "Emmanuel. We've been expecting you."

"I know," I said. "I met Seth on the way, and Abel a few days ago. Look, I want to talk to Adam, but I hope I'm not troubling you."

But then a clear, dignified voice told me it was no trouble at all. I looked up to see a venerable, dignified man emerging from the cave. He was wearing a large, tiger skin robe and a beaver skin hat. His large brown eyes penetrated my soul as I stood transfixed. By his very bearing, this man commanded respect. I knew it had to be Adam.

Adam smiled graciously, walked over to where I was standing and embraced me warmly. I felt flooded with a feeling of love and comfort. I felt safe in Adam's presence, and all of my worries left me. I forgot about all of the concerns on my mind, the questions that perplexed me, the problems I wished to confront him with. I even forgot that Eve, the most beautiful woman in the world, was standing there. I wanted to speak, but emotion choked me. I just let Adam hold me in his embrace, I buried my face in his robe, and I wept. He comforted me softly as I knelt down before him, held his hand in mine and begged him to forgive me for my insolence and the way I had treated Abel. He lovingly reassured me, told me that I had nothing to worry about, that all was already forgiven, and that I had done very well to come. He lifted me up and bade me sit down by the fire, where he sat down beside me. I continued to weep as the strong and mighty man patiently observed me. Could it not be, he gently observed, that I had brought all of this sadness and confusion upon myself? Could not a change of attitude, a slight change of heart be the solution to all of the problems that oppressed me? I looked at him, and he was smiling at me radiantly. His countenance looked like the sun shining in its noon-tide glory. Then the emotion that overwhelmed me began to surge and spill out of my mouth. I told Adam all of my problems, all of my worries, explaining the cause of all of my anxieties. I hadn't realized it, but I knew that my heart was full of fear, and I was ignorant of the solution. Eden was no longer a place of comfort to me. I had never missed my father or my mother before, or even wished that I had known them, but now the consciousness that I was but an orphan dawned on me. I had never had a protector or a comforter, someone to guide me and direct me upon the right paths of life. I had never known truth or morality. My friends fought for me because they felt like it, I fought my enemies because I felt like it. I had made love to many women in my young life, all because it was pleasurable. But now I knew that I felt so empty. No matter how many beautiful women I had sex with, it could not satisfy. I felt abandoned, cold and alone. And now this matter with Sarah. Was she the solution to my problems? Did Adam really want me to stay with her forever?

Adam smiled, pulled me to my feet, and in a few gentle words he relieved my perplexities. He told me that the answer to all of my problems was love, a bounty I had never known, something that he was showing me now. By the time I left him, he confidently said, I would know all about love, my heart would be full of it, and I would share it with Sarah. Yes, he said, faithfulness to Sarah would indeed prove the solution to all of my troubles, because the problem, he said, was not with the rest of Eden, but it was with myself. It was to myself that I had to look for answers, because within myself I would find the question. My soul, he said, had become a wilderness, full of wild beasts and useless weeds, a jungle that only love could tame into a beautiful and pleasant garden. Turn to love, he assured me, and I would change, and then all would be well.

After saying these things and calming me somewhat, Adam arose and gently bid me follow him into the cave. So I rose and followed him into the cave from which I had first seen him emerge. The cave was about fifty feet deep, and it was illumined inside by bright torches which had been placed in holes carved in the walls. In the center of the cave, there was a cavernous room, lit by firelight, whose ground was covered in deerskins and in the center of which a sumptuous feast of fruits, rice, grains, vegetables, and several kinds of meat had been laid. There were also cups of pomegranate juice and apple juice. Adam bade me be seated, and he sat down himself. I asked him politely if Eve or Seth would be joining us, and Adam said that this time was reserved for him and me alone. So I gratefully took a sip of my drink, and began eating. I hadn't realized how hungry I was, but then I noticed that Adam and I must have been talking for hours. The food was incredibly refreshing, and I had never enjoyed such a rich repast. The meat had been prepared differently than I had ever tasted it, and it was absolutely delicious.

As I ate, Adam talked, and explained to me many things, patiently expounding the answers to questions I had never thought of asking. As he talked, the solutions to the problems of life seemed simple and easy of accomplishment. Everything I had worried about before, that had caused me so much concern, anxiety and fear, seemed completely insignificant and irrelevant. I marveled at how ignorant I had been, how steeped in darkness, and I admired Adam's love and knowledge with an enthusiasm I could not suppress. I became aware that a radiant smile had illumined my own face as I listened to Adam explain the mysteries of life. I was not dimly aware of the hours passing by, but by the time Adam had finished talking the night had come and gone, and it was already after dawn. Sleep had departed from me that night, and I was invigorated by a new power with which Adam's spirit and words had filled my soul.

Finally Adam asked me to follow him out of the cave. Seth was sitting outside by the river, and talking with him was Eve. They saw us approach and both got up to meet us. Eve smiled at me and embraced her husband. Adam remarked that I was a very pure hearted and receptive soul and that I had learned much from him that night. Then Eve said that I had to stay with them a few more days. I happily agreed. I could never have enough time beside Adam, although I knew I had to get back to Sarah as well.

After we talked for a few minutes, Eve took Adam by the hand and led him inside one of the larger huts. Seth asked me if I wanted to sleep.

"I'm not tired," I said, "And sitting in the presence of Adam was like a dream. Indeed, I am entirely refreshed. All the sleep in the world could not have imparted to me so much strength."

"Such power is spiritual," Seth replied. "When the spirit takes control of the body, one is capable of anything."

"I knew nothing of spiritual matters before," I told Seth.

Seth nodded. "Eden is not a spiritual land," he said. "It is a land of bestiality and ignorance. My father has always said that we do not belong here."

"Then where do we belong?" I asked.

"It is not a matter of place," Seth replied. "But in a matter of speaking, we belong in the realm of the heart. At the very least, we have to use our minds and intelligence. We have to be responsible. We need to know the difference between good and evil, right and wrong. At present, no one in Eden has any morals. No one, that is, except for my father."

"Your father can change things for the better," I said, "just as he has changed me."

"He is planning to do just that," Seth said.

I stayed with Adam, Eve and Seth two more days. I cannot begin to express the amount of kindness and love that Adam bestowed upon me. He truly filled me with enough spiritual strength for a lifetime. By the end of my stay, my entire life had changed. My views, my attitude, my outlook, my ideas about right and wrong were different. I now had a reason to hope and a purpose to live for. I couldn't wait to get back and share my new knowledge, my new self, with Sarah.

7

This is now bone of my bones
And flesh of my flesh;
She shall be called Woman,
Because she was taken out of Man.

Genesis 2:23

"Sarah?"

It had been eleven days since I had left her alone with Heber. Dawn was just beginning to break with streaks of red and orange over the horizon as I walked toward the hut.

"Emmanuel?" Heber came to the door of the hut. "You're back."

"Where's Sarah?" I asked my friend.

Sarah appeared out of the hut as well. "Emmanuel?"

"Sarah!" I held out my arms. Sarah ran toward me and jumped into them. I wrapped her in my embrace.

I stood there, enclosing her in my arms, and I didn't want to stop. Eventually Sarah pulled back and looked at me with curious eyes. "Emmanuel, did you find Adam?"

I smiled at her, picking her up and twirling her in the air. When I put her back down, I kissed her on the forehead and wrapped her in my arms again.

She blushed, her cheeks hot against mine.

"Emmanuel, who is your guest?" Heber was looking at a young blonde man, of medium height, average build, and a handsome face. "I am Seth, son of Adam," the young man replied. He was my age, maybe a year younger. His voice rang out confidently in the early morning.

"What is a son of Adam doing here?" Sarah asked me, wonder in her eyes.

"I didn't know Adam had another son," Heber said.

"My father has sent me on a special mission," Seth replied.

I held Sarah by the arms and looked her in the eyes. "You wouldn't believe what Adam has planned," I said to her. "What has happened with us is only the beginning."

Sarah didn't understand. "What happened between us, Emmanuel?"

"We are together forever now, Sarah," I said.

"So you've done it? Adam has convinced you to take her to wife?" Heber said.

Seth spoke for me. "My father hasn't convinced him of anything. He just helped Emmanuel understand what he already knew."

"What did you know, Emmanuel?" Sarah asked.

"That you're the mother of my child, Sarah," I said tenderly. "That you need me to protect you, not just now, but for the rest of your life. That we are to raise our children together, not just for a year, but until they grow to adulthood. That you need more than just physical love from me, you need a commitment, a connection."

"And you have agreed to this?" Sarah asked gently. "You don't want to be free anymore?"

I turned to Seth, and put a hand on his shoulder. He smiled at me.

"I didn't know what freedom was," I said to Sarah. "Then I met Adam. He showed me that I'm more than the man I thought I was."

Sarah looked confused. "I don't understand, Emmanuel."

I smiled at her with a joy I could not suppress. "We have a lot of time to talk about it, Sarah," I said. "We have walked a long distance without stopping. I am sure our guest wants to rest for a few hours."

"You are tired too, Emmanuel," Seth said. "We should both rest a little."

"Where is Seth going to sleep?" Sarah asked.

"I'll sleep outside, under the sky," Seth replied.

"Seth, that won't do," I said. "You're a son of Adam."

But Seth insisted. He didn't want to be a burden to us, and he said that he didn't need to be comfortable to be happy.

Heber said his goodbyes to us. I thanked him for staying with Sarah before he left.

Then Sarah and I went inside the hut. "I will sleep a little, Sarah," I said to her. "But I want to hold you in my arms while I do so."

"I've missed you, Emmanuel," Sarah said. Who was this girl, who cared so deeply for me for no apparent reason?

I lay down with her, and fell asleep with her in my arms.

When I woke up, Sarah was looking at me and smiling. I kissed her and held her close. She breathed into my chest as she squeezed me back.

"You've been asleep a long time," she said to me.

"It was a long journey," I replied. Then I remembered our guest. "Where's Seth?"

"Still outside, I guess."

"I'm going to go see if he needs anything," I said. I got up, stretched and went outside. It was midday, and the sun was out in a cloudless sky. Seth was cooking vegetables by the fire.

"My mother's recipe," Seth said to me as I sat down beside him. "I thought you and Sarah would like it."

"Smells good," I said.

Sarah came out as well. "Seth, you didn't have to cook," she said.

But Seth only smiled. "I am here to serve you, not to be served," he said.

Sarah wrinkled her nose. "You said your father has sent you on a special mission," she said. "What is it?"

"I think it's ready," Seth said, taking the vegetables off the fire. He made a plate for Sarah, one for me, and one for himself. "I hope you like it."

I took a bite of a carrot. "It's good," I said. I enjoyed it.

"Family is important," Seth replied. "Father is distressed that people have ignored it for so long. He says it's time for Eden to change."

"And you are going to change it?" Sarah asked. She seemed doubtful.

"I am going to try," Seth replied. "I want to wake people up. Help them to see the truth. They are living like animals."

Sarah looked at me. "What was that you said before to me? That you are more than the man you thought you were?"

"We all are, Sarah," I replied. "We are more than just bodies. We have souls."

"Souls are what separate us from animals," Seth replied. "It is a teaching of my father."

"What's a soul?" Sarah asked.

"A soul is who we really are, on the inside. It's different than our body. If we lost an arm or a leg, we would still be who we are. Likewise, if we lost our whole bodies, or if we died, we would still be ourselves. We would live on. We are souls."

"So how does knowing that change us?" Sarah asked.

"Because we have to do more than just live for pleasure," I replied. "We have a purpose for being here in Eden. We have to live meaningful lives, love each other with more than just physical love. We have to care for each other, be there for each other. Not just make love to each other one night and then forget about each other the next."

"And the violence that has been increasing lately has deeply distressed my father," Seth replied. "He wants it to stop. He wants men to start acting responsibly and being good to each other."

"And he started with us," Sarah said.

"Adam has been wanting to act for some time," Seth replied. "When the argument between Emmanuel and Morag started, he knew it was time. He told Emmanuel to be faithful to you because he knew Emmanuel was a good man, and that you were good for him."

"Adam seemed to know me," I said to Sarah. "He knew my heart, even better than I knew it myself. Like I said, he helped me realize what I already knew. That I loved you."

"You didn't talk or act like you loved me before," Sarah said.

"I wasn't in touch with my heart or my feelings, Sarah," I said sadly. "I was living like a savage. We all were. Adam helped me to see the error of my ways, that I was more than what I thought I was. He filled my heart with the same warmth and goodness that you knew was always there."

"Emmanuel was a receptive soul," Seth replied. "When he met Adam, he was transformed by his compassion, wisdom and love."

"And Adam had all of the highest praise for you, Sarah," I said. "He told me that you are a special girl, that there is no one else in Eden like you, and that I should cherish you carefully. And that is something else that I also knew."

Sarah smiled. "What of the others? Do you think they will take so kindly to Adam's message?"

Seth looked serious. "My mother doesn't think so. She says that the people of Eden aren't ready to hear what Adam has to say. She believes they will just ignore his teachings, or rebel against him. But my father says that he has to try. He has to give people the chance to be better."

"Adam has sent Seth to travel throughout Eden, and bring people the message Adam wants them to hear," I said.

"Why doesn't Adam do this teaching himself?" Sarah asked.

"I am young and unmarried," Seth replied. "My father wants to stay with my mother so that people can see in his life an example of what he wants to teach. He also wants to be there to receive any visitors who want to come to him. Those who are truly receptive and willing, with pure hearts, will always be able to hear his words and be changed by them."

"Seth is up to the task," I told Sarah. "He's a fine young man, a worthy son of his father. He has great wisdom, as you will soon come to know."

"I will stay with the two of you for a few days, telling you all I know about families," Seth replied. "Then I will journey through the rest of Eden, speaking to anyone who will listen."

We talked all day and deep into the night, sitting next to the bright, crackling fire.

"The way we've been living in Eden is not good," Seth said gravely. "Living for passion only—where has it gotten us? We are supposed to live long, full lives, but there has been so much killing and death lately that people rarely get old anymore. And all of this killing and senseless violence—why? Because our passions are ruling our minds and bodies. Our souls are on the back burner, while we destroy all that is good in ourselves and in everyone around us. We live only for pleasure, and what happens when someone else comes in the way of our pleasure?" Seth took a deep breath. "Most of your friends and family are dead now, Sarah, and it's all because people valued their own pride more than each other. Adam wants the people of Eden to rise above such a degraded condition and find their own nobility." Sarah studied Seth's face, illuminated by the orange glow of the fire. "And having men and women choose one partner for the rest of their lives—that is going to solve all of this?"

"Look at what it's done for me, Sarah," I said. "Deciding to dedicate myself to your love has revolutionized my life. I suddenly have a purpose now; I'm not living only for myself."

Seth nodded. "The purpose in this teaching of Adam is that people should learn what care and love truly mean. When we treat each other like savages, only violence and suffering result. We are left cold and uncared for, not knowing what it means to value another, to love another. The people of Eden know how to pleasure each other—that is all well and good. But what is the difference between sex with someone you do not care about, and violence against someone who has wronged you? Passion is passion, no matter what form it takes. It is ruling the lives of all of the people of Eden. There is a wide difference between passion and love. When you truly love another, that love isn't confined only to them. It spreads to those around you, too. A man whose heart is full of love will never hurt, kill or betray another, whether known to him or a stranger, whether a friend or a foe."

"And can I really say I love you if I am with you one day and forget you the next?" I told Sarah. "Did you feel like I loved you when I didn't want to be with you for a year?"

"No," Sarah said.

"And even now, I cannot show you and our child true love unless I vow to be with you for the rest of your lives, and make good on that promise."

"A child changes things between a man and a woman," Seth said. "It is an expression of the love two people share, but that child needs love too. It gives its parents the chance to create a space filled with the same love that created it, where it can grow and be nurtured. This space is a home. The love that is meant to fill a home isn't for the child only, it is a chance for a man and woman to grow also in the spirit of care and love."

"I can feel that love from you now, Emmanuel," Sarah said to me. "You are so much different than you were before."

I nodded. "The change you see in me was Adam's doing," I said. "I feel invigorated by a new spirit. I was like one dead before, now I am alive."

I smiled. "I promise to bring you joy for the rest of your life, Sarah." She smiled back. "I know you will, Emmanuel."

"Eden has been living in an eternal childhood," Seth replied. "Adam believes that now the time of its adolescence has begun. It is time for people to begin to take responsibility for their lives and their actions."

"Don't you see, Sarah?" I said. "Eden can become so much more than it is now."

"But the people of Eden have to make that choice," Seth said. "Our lives are now full of pleasure, but our hearts are empty and tragedy abounds. We can exchange that pleasure with joy, trade the passion that characterizes our lives with a love that means much more than sex. We are now living in nature, which supplies all of our needs; but we can rise above nature. My father believes that the people of Eden can build a society, a civilization. We can work together and cooperate to rise out of our darkness and walk into the light."

Seth stayed with us a few more days, and then he left. When he did, Sarah and I discussed the adventure that he had ahead of him.

"Do you think he'll succeed?" Sarah asked. "Do you think the people of Eden will listen to him?"

"I don't know," I replied. "The message he brings is hard to accept. He wants people to be responsible, to abandon the pursuit of pleasure and unbridled passion. I don't know how they will receive that."

"I'm afraid the people of Eden won't be like you and I, Emmanuel," Sarah said.

I held her close. "I was able to change because I had you to look forward to," I said. "But tell me, why did you choose me? You seemed to truly love me before Adam or anyone else told you to." Sarah kissed me on the cheek. "Seth told me something before he left," she said. "He said that when Adam saw the unconditional love and forgiveness I had for you, even after all that you did to my family, he decided that Eden was ready to grow up. Adam saw evidence that the people of Eden would be able to make commitments to each other and create families."

"But where did this love of yours come from?" I asked her.

She gave me a hug. "I was made for you, Emmanuel."

8

Now the serpent was more cunning than any beast of the field which the Lord God had made.

Genesis 3:1

After Seth left, Sarah and I made love for hours under the open sky. Eventually we fell asleep in each other's arms, and when we awoke we made love again under the moonlight. It didn't get old, making love to Sarah. If anything it got more pleasurable. There was something different about it, being with a woman I would never leave, a woman who would never leave me. There was something more satisfying, a warmth that filled the heart as well as the body. I became aware that there was a need deep inside of me, a need for love, for affection, for connection, for commitment; a need that Sarah filled, but that I hadn't even known I had.

I asked Sarah if she had felt the same way.

"Unlike most of the people in Eden, I always had a family who looked out for me. You saw that. So I knew what it was like to be thought of, cared for, protected. When Morag and my brothers and uncles died fighting you, I wondered if there would be anyone else, or if I would be left alone to fend for myself. I was frightened and sad. But you came for me. You agreed to stay with me and protected me. And now you're going to be with me forever."

"Whose protection did you enjoy more?" I asked. "Morag's, or mine?"

Sarah smiled. "Yours, of course."

"Morag couldn't make love to you," I said. "I can."

"A lover and a protector," Sarah replied. "You're everything to me."

"And you'll never grow tired of my love?" I asked.

"Never," Sarah whispered. She was standing before me, in the first light of dawn, her arms around my back. She kissed me on the neck. I kissed her bare shoulder, and then lifted her up and carried her into the tent.

Sarah's pulse had quickened, and her skin was hot against mine.

"Make love to me again," she said. I lay her on her back and made love to her as she moaned softly beneath me.

That was how it was between Sarah and me every day. We made love, we ate, we slept; we talked underneath the moonlight; in the mornings we'd go out into the orchards and fields of berries and flowers around our home and pick fruits or enjoy the beauty of our surroundings. Occasionally we ran into others who were out walking together or living nearby. Sometimes Heber visited us in our home. But Sarah and I were taken with each other; we didn't need anyone else for company, and when others were present we hardly noticed them. We were so wrapped up in one another.

Both of us had made love with many others in our young lives, but neither of us had been in love before. It was different. I never grew tired of her. And she, knowing that she could trust me, opened up to me in a way I had never known a girl do before. She was like a young and delicate flower that came into full bloom every time she stood before me. And I loved and cherished her with all my heart. I knew that I would never leave or forsake her, never go back on my promise. Every time I held her in my arms I told her that it would be forever.

"Even death cannot separate us," I said to her. "Adam has said that our souls go on after we die. And the vows we have made to each other are immortal, too."

Our love became stronger, more fierce. I knew that I would never let anybody hurt her; and if I would ever have to fight for her honor, I wouldn't die doing it like Morag had done. I would defend her with strength and wisdom, and I knew nothing could stop our love. I didn't want anybody else, I didn't need anything else. Sarah was enough for me.

Adam had put this love into my heart; he had made me ready for it, opened me up to it. I silently thanked him every time I lay eyes on Sarah. People were right to admire and honor the man. He had more than just wisdom; his words were moved by an intangible spirit of truth that brought life to those who heard him.

As the months wore on, the child in Sarah's stomach grew larger. I would lie there with my head on her womb, listening to the child kick and turn. Sarah's smile was radiant as I showed my marks of affection for the child, her eyes flashing with joy and pride as she anticipated the family we would become.

When the baby came near to term, we stopped making love. I would hold Sarah at night, promising her that we would have a healthy child. I would go out and hunt deer or wild hogs and cook for her. I'd bring her fruits and vegetables and water from the stream. She would mostly stay at home. I made her relax.

The girl was still attractive to me though. I'd drink in the sight of her every time I saw her. I'd tell her how beautiful she was to me. "I saw Eve, and she's as beautiful as they say, but even she doesn't compare to you in my eyes."

"You don't mean that," Sarah would reply.

"Yes I do," I'd say, "and I'll prove it to you once the child is born."

"Prove it to me now."

"You know I can't do that."

So I'd kiss her, and stroke her hair, and tell her jokes to make her laugh.

Eventually it came time for Sarah to give birth. Her water broke one morning shortly after breakfast, and she started having weak contractions. I went to fetch two old women who could help us with the birth. They were living alone in their huts, structures which younger men had built for them, and they ate wild fruits and vegetables. They were happy for the change in their daily routine, which seemed to have grown stale.

On the way back to our home, they complimented me on the dedication I had shown to Sarah.

"When that trouble with her brothers first started, no one thought that any good would come out of this for any of you," said the older woman. Her name was Herut. "When Cain beat you in that wrestling match, I was sure that you would resent having to care for the girl. But then when news came that you had taken her to wife, as Adam had done with Eve, everyone was surprised. They say the girl always believed you would be there for her. I thought she was a dreamer."

"I found Sarah's convictions strange too, at first," I said. "I was a man who lived only for pleasure, who shirked all thought of responsibility. But Adam has shown me the error of my former ways. I have changed now, Herut."

"I know, Emmanuel," the old woman said. Her skin was wrinkled but soft on her face, her hair long but grey. Then she looked down at the ground, sadly. "If only the young people of Eden would be more like you. They say the young son of Adam has had a terrible time in his travels."

"You have news of Seth?" I asked. "I haven't heard of him since he left many months ago."

Apparently the old women were better informed of the happenings around Eden than I was.

"He has been visiting young and old alike, men and women, telling them to change their lives. He has been preaching about marriage and commitment, saying that true happiness only comes with dedication and commitment. As you can imagine, the young people do not want to hear any of it."

"So his efforts have not met with success, then?" I asked.

"They say he has made many friends among the people he has spoken to," Herut said. "Everyone admires his father, and they like the young man too. But they haven't taken him seriously. No matter how seriously he exhorts them, they laugh his words away and invite him to join in their revelry."

"I am sure he refuses, of course," I said.
The other woman, Netta, had kept quiet for some time, but now she spoke up.

"They say the youngest son of Adam is a virgin. He has never known a woman."

"That doesn't surprise me," I said. "He really believes in his father's ideals."

"It's good for a young man, if you'd ask me," Netta said thoughtfully. "You never saw me in my day, but I was beautiful. All the young men wanted me. They fought for me, even killed for me. And all of the love and pleasure I received in return, where has it gotten me? I am an old woman now, my beauty is gone, and I live alone. The men I knew, that wasn't love. If it was, at least one of them would still be around. But they are all gone."

"It is sad, Netta," I replied. We were arriving at the clearing. "I have promised Sarah that will never happen to her. The two of us will grow old together, even die together."

"If the young people of Eden knew what we old ones knew, they wouldn't be so quick to dismiss Adam's words," Herut said gravely.

"They are reckless and ignorant. They are only hurting themselves with their loose ways, even though they do not know it."

"I can see that Seth has at least won the two of you over to his cause," I replied. We had arrived at the hut. I led the two old ladies inside.

Sarah was lying on her back, sweat on her face. "Emmanuel," she said. "The baby is coming."

Herut and Netta went to work. Herut had brought a special cloth made from the cocoon of the silk worm as a gift for the child, and she used it to mop Sarah's forehead. Netta felt Sarah's stomach.

"The child is doing finely," the old woman said. "It will be out soon."
Sarah started to scream as the pain got more intense. Herut held her hand and told her to breathe.

"Push," Netta said. "The baby needs your help to come out."

I stood by the doorway to the hut, watching as Sarah pushed. The process took a long time. The pain Sarah felt would come and go. Several times I went out to bring the three women water and food. As I waited, I began to get worried. "Is everything alright?" I asked Herut.

"The girl is fine, and the child will be healthy. It is just a little while longer," the old woman said.

Finally the baby came. Sarah screamed as it fell into Netta's outstretched arms.

"It is a girl," Netta said. "A beautiful child."

I gave Herut a basin of water, with which she washed the child. After the newborn was clean, Herut wrapped it in the silk cloth and handed it to Sarah.

"The child of your love," the old woman said.

"The child of my dreams," Sarah replied. She was smiling broadly and held her daughter close. I came up to her and kissed first Sarah, and then the baby on the forehead.

"I'm so proud of you, Sarah," I said softly.

"Thanking you for being here, Emmanuel," Sarah said.

I felt a finger on my shoulder. It was Herut. "Emmanuel," she said. "You have a visitor."
"At this hour?" I asked. But when I turned around, sure enough, there was a man standing in the doorway. I instantly recognized the long blonde hair and handsome face as Seth's. He had grown a beard since I had seen him last, and his clothes were worn and travel-stained.

"Seth," Sarah said.

The young man beamed at the sight of the woman with her child. "So she is here," Seth replied. "The child that started it all."

"Seth, we had better go outside," I said. I turned to Sarah. "I will come back in a few minutes. Netta and Herut will tend to you."

"Okay," Sarah said.

I led Seth out of the hut. There, in the starlight, I embraced him. "My friend," I said warmly. "It has been so long."

"I haven't had as good a time in Eden as I had with you and Sarah," Seth replied. He looked serious and a little sad. "The other people I visited didn't receive me so well."

"I heard your message met with deaf ears," I said. I picked up a log and threw it into the fire, which was dying down. "We have food. Are you hungry?"

"Yes, a little," Seth replied.

He told me of his experiences while he ate. "People respect my father, and they were glad to receive a visit from a son of Adam," Seth said. "But when I spoke to them about commitment and purpose, it was as if they didn't even hear me. They patted me on the back and laughed, and told me to lighten up. No matter how much I admonished them, they wouldn't believe that I was serious."

"That is how Eden is," I told Seth. "The people do not live like your parents. They have no cares, no responsibilities. Why willingly accept hardships when they can live for pleasure?"
"Because hardships inevitably come, Emmanuel. People aren't young forever. They are giving up an eternity of joy and happiness for a fleeting desire. Their days come and go, and they are lucky if they even live to old age. You yourself have seen what the people of Eden will do to each other over the smallest trifle. My father believed that the people of Eden could be more. He thought they would come around. But my mother always said they wouldn't listen."

"Did anyone listen to your words, Seth? Anyone at all?"

"Like I said, I made a lot of friends," Seth replied. "But no one felt moved to changed their lives or behavior. You and Sarah are still the only ones to have married."

I was worried by Seth's reply. Sarah and I had been the only ones?

9

So when the woman saw that the tree was good for food, that it was pleasant to the eyes, and a tree desirable to make one wise, she took of its fruit and ate. She also gave to her husband with her, and he ate.

Genesis 3:6

Seth stayed with us for a few days. He constantly praised the child's beauty, which he said was beyond compare; so Sara and I named her Nava, which means 'beautiful'. I would cradle Nava in my arms and tell her how special she was. "Men have died over you, and your mother and I came together just to love you. Something tells me that men will fight over you again in the future, but I want you to know that I will always be here to protect you. No man will get his hands on my Nava unless I deem him good enough."

Sara would laugh. "What man in Eden would you deem good enough for your daughter?"

I would turn serious. "There are not many men worthy of her. But it is my hope that in the coming generation there will be some who are different from their fathers."

But Seth was sad. "The people of Eden do not want to change," he said. "I hoped that by now there would be a multitude ready to grow up and be responsible."

Seth left to inform his parents of the results of his travels. He was sure they would be disappointed, but I felt that Adam would know what to do. He wasn't a man to fail in his intentions. So I helped Sarah raise Nava as I waited to see what would become of Eden. I would hunt and gather food for my wife and daughter, and cook for them every day. I fashioned clothes and blankets for them from beaver and squirrel furs and from the skins of deer and oxen. We would receive many visits from friends and acquaintances around Eden, who were curious to see the lives of the only ones who had followed Adam's advice. They were surprised to see that we were happy and content. We didn't miss the wild life that characterized the rest of Eden. From the vantage point of the new light that shone upon our lives, our past lives were filled with darkness; and our old ways were death compared with the new life that the teachings of Adam had given us. I patiently explained to my friends and visitors what the companionship of Sarah meant to me, and I told them that if they only knew the comfort and security that a meaningful relationship could bring, they would stop looking upon each other as the objects of lust and passion.

The presence of Nava brought Sarah and me closer together. We now had something to do with our time together other than make love; we had a mutual purpose that we worked together to accomplish. Raising our daughter was something that we both devoted our efforts to. I was happy to see the great love that Sarah had for Nava, and Sarah was delighted to witness the priority which her and her daughter's well-being held in my life.

Nava was several months old when we unexpectedly received a tall, dark and handsome visitor whom I instantly recognized as Cain, the eldest son of Adam. I greeted him and introduced him to Sarah and my newborn child.

"Let us just say that I'm happy you're willing to do what it takes to win a fight," I said, placing an arm on Cain's shoulder. The antagonism that had characterized our brutal wrestling-match was long forgotten. I was grateful to Adam and all his sons for helping to bring my family together. Cain, too, seemed to have completely forgotten the cause of the anger that had filled him that day at the river.

"My friend Emmanuel," Cain said, his eyebrows raised like lofty falcons, his glance sharp and penetrating. "I can see that you have built a new life for yourself with Sarah, a girl who once caused you so much trouble."

"I was to blame for the trouble surrounding Sarah's family," I replied, holding Sarah's hand. "I am only grateful that your family intervened."

Sarah laughed. "You'd have to have been crazy to believe in Morag's dream like he did," she said. "You were only doing what you thought was right and following your heart."

"My heart led me astray, Sarah," I said. I took Nava from my wife's arms and held her before Cain. "Isn't she beautiful?" I said. "She is going to need strong brothers to protect her from the eager young men."
"Seth told us about the child the two of you have been blessed with," Cain replied. He reached out to hold the child, and I handed her to him.

"You are the future of Eden," he said to the baby, whom he rocked back and forth. When Nava began to cry, Cain handed her back to her mother.

"She must be hungry," Sarah said. She took Nava back into the hut. I told Seth to be seated. "Are you hungry?" I asked him.

"I've eaten on the way," Cain replied.

"What news from Adam?" I asked him.

Cain smiled, and looked at me with feelings of excitement. "That's what I'm here to talk to you about. There's been a development."
I studied him. "And you seem quite pleased. What is it?"

Cain smiled again. "When Seth returned with news of his travels in Eden, my father took it all in stride. He said that people are free to make their own choices. But my mother wasn't as willing to let it go. She was frustrated by the insolence and carelessness of the people, and I think it angered her a little. She wasn't patient like my father." Cain paused and looked at me gleefully. "So?" I asked. "What did your mother say?"

Cain continued. "Eve said that things can't just continue to go the way they are now. She said my father had to do something."

"What did she have in mind?" I asked.

"My father thought that my mother wanted him to speak to the people himself. But she was thinking along entirely different lines. 'It is just as I thought, the people of Eden will never listen to reason and common sense,' Eve said. 'But they will bow before a leader who rules with authority.'"

"But Eden doesn't have any leaders," I replied.
"My mother knew that," Cain said. "But she thought that it was time for that to change. She told my father to gather an army from among his supporters in Eden and to conquer the land in the name of moral development and responsibility. She said that he could become the first king that Eden had ever known, and with that power establish law and order in the land. Physical force, she said, was needed in order to make the people of Eden submit to his laws."

Cain was smiling broadly and there was a slightly wild gleam in his eyes. I wasn't sure I shared his excitement. "What did your father say to this?" I replied, slightly worried.

"My father thought about it, as any reasonable person would," Cain replied, sobering slightly. "After a few days, he decided that my mother was right. There was no other way to ensure that the people of Eden wouldn't destroy themselves with their foolishness. The only right course, he declared, was for him to become king."

Cain stood up. He reached his hand out to me, and I took it and stoop up with him. He directed my attention to the sky. "Look at where we live," he said, gazing around him. "The land supplies all our needs, but even the land is nourished by the sun shining from the heavens above it. At night, the moon and the stars guide us and enable us to see. What would we be if we weren't watched over by these brilliant orbs? The people of Eden need a king, a higher authority, to watch over them from above. Without the light of his law and justice, how will they live? You must help me raise my father to the throne."

I was concerned. "I don't know about this, Cain. I'm not sure how Eden will take to having Adam proclaim himself as king."

"The people of Eden love my father," Cain replied, unfazed. "They will be glad to raise him up as their king."

Sarah came out of the hut with Nava sleeping in her arms. "She was tired," she said.

I gently stroked the child's face. "So Adam wants all of this so that a child like Nava will be protected," I said to Cain.
"You know that Eden isn't a good environment for children, Emmanuel," Cain replied. "What are they learning as they grow among us? They learn respect neither for themselves nor for those around them."

I sighed, turning to Sarah. "Adam wants to become the king of all of Eden," I said. "He thinks that if the people won't listen to his admonitions, the only way to make things better is to bring order through force."

Sarah looked at Cain, surprised. "Is your father serious?" she asked.

"My father and mother both agree, it is the only way. I came here to ask Emmanuel to help us raise an army. Abel and Seth are already traveling throughout Eden with that very purpose."

I took the sleeping baby from Sarah's arms, and held it closely. It opened its eyes and yawned, smiling when it saw me. "My year isn't over yet," I said. "I still have to stay with Sarah and the baby."

"You're married to Sarah now, Emmanuel," Cain objected. "It's different between you. You don't only have to stay with her for a year, you will stay with her forever. She knows that. I am sure she will understand if you leave her for a while for a matter as important as this."

Sarah nodded. "It's for Nava's future, Emmanuel," she said. "It's for all of our futures. I will be alright here if you go."

"What do you say, Emmanuel?" Cain asked hopefully.

I looked at my daughter. "I know things need to change around Eden," I said finally. "But I need time to think about it."

I will stay here for the night," Cain said. "If you decide to come with me, we will leave together tomorrow. If not, I will set out alone."

I decided to help Cain and the sons of Adam raise their army. Sarah and Nava had all of their needs provided for at our home, and there was nothing to pose a threat to their safety. So Cain and I set out from the clearing at dawn with a single objective in mind: to raise as many supporters of Adam as we could to form an army. The most devoted of them would serve Adam permanently as soldiers and guards of his new kingdom.

"Abel and Seth are calling the people together to a spot known to us about three day's journey from here," Cain said. "We will have a general meeting there in three weeks. That is where we will call upon volunteers for our army."

"So I take it we are to gather people and inform them of the meeting?" I said.

"Exactly," Cain replied.

We went first to Heber's hut. He was cooking deer by the fire. I told him that the sons of Adam were gathering people for a great announcement they were to make at an appointed place, and Heber agreed to come with us and inform people of the event. "Anything to break the monotony of life," he said.

We traveled around Eden, telling people that the sons of Adam were calling everyone to an important meeting. Cain told me in no uncertain terms to maintain strict silence about the purpose of the gathering, and he refused to disclose the secret to anyone himself. The mystery surrounding the event would attract more curiosity, he said, and he also didn't want anyone to hear about what was coming until the right time. Almost everyone was curious about what was happening, and most of those who didn't follow us outright agreed to meet us at the appointed time. We soon had a large crowd behind us consisting of men and women of all ages who admired Cain and who wanted to hear what the sons of Adam had to say. The people didn't restrain themselves around Cain. Every night men and women from the crowd would sleep together, often choosing multiple partners and seemingly forgetful of the values to which Seth had so passionately exhorted them only months ago. Cain held his peace as these events transpired; the time for bidding the people change their conduct, he confidently told me, would come soon enough.

Three weeks after Cain and I set out, we arrived at a large meadow between two mighty rivers, filled with flowers of all colors and bound on each side by rolling hills. There were over five hundred people with us, and a crowd of thousands awaited us when we got there. The people cheered when they saw Cain, and Abel and Seth came out to meet us.

"You are late, Cain," Abel said after he greeted us. "The people are waiting for our announcement. The appointed time has come. Do you want to speak, or should I?"

"I am the better speaker, Abel," Cain said. He scanned the faces of the people in the meadow. "More have come than I expected. I will address them from the hill, while you and Seth stand by my side."

The three brothers ascended the nearby hill as I moved to the front of the crowd. An hour later, the people suddenly became quiet. Cain was preparing to speak.
Cain held a large ox-skin towel aloft over his hands. There seemed to be something moving beneath it. A loud gasp went throughout the crowd as Cain dropped the towel to the ground and the people saw what that thing was. A large serpent, as thick as a thigh and over ten feet long, was resting in Cain's arms. It hissed as it wrapped itself around Cain's shoulders and raised its head above Cain's.

"People of Eden!" Cain announced. You could have heard a pin drop, it had gotten so quiet. "You may think that I am in danger with this large serpent crawling about me. But that danger is nothing compared to the danger imposed by the Serpent poisoning the life of the people of Eden. You know of which serpent I speak. The serpent of violence, the serpent of barbarity, the serpent of lawlessness and unbridled passion."

A murmur went throughout the crowd as Cain threw the serpent to the ground. It lifted its head and hissed at him. Abel gave Cain a hatchet with a sharpened rock tied to one end. Cain hacked at the serpent, severing its head. Then he chopped wildly at the rest of the serpent's body, cutting it to pieces. Blood sprayed all over his face and hands as the crowd watched in silence.

Cain stood up again and stared at the people. "What do you do to stop a serpent?" he asked. "You do not talk to it, you do not reason with it, you do not indulge its appetites. I'll tell you what you do to a serpent. You kill it."

The people murmured their approval. Cain continued. "You all are living like animals," he said, "and animals are prey for serpents. You are destroying yourselves and those around you, although you do not know it. My father, Adam, has decided that things must change. You are not children any more, and you are not beasts. You are men and women. The time has come for you to start acting like it."

There was dead silence among the crowd. No one moved.

"Eden must be civilized," Cain said. "You all know what you need and want. You want a leader. You want a king, who can guide you and help you discern the difference between right and wrong."
A murmur went throughout the crowd. This was not what people were expecting. Some people cursed Cain, while others shouted for him to continue.

"My father, Adam, will be your king," Cain shouted. "The purpose of this meeting is to raise an army to establish his kingdom, the first kingdom that Eden has ever known. All those who wish to participate as soldiers in Adam's army may stay. The rest of you can go home."

10

Then the eyes of both of them were opened, and they knew that they were naked; and they sewed fig leaves together and made themselves coverings

Genesis 3:7

So the Lord God said to the serpent: "Because you have done this, you are cursed more than all cattle, and more than every beast of the field; on your belly you shall go, and you shall eat dust all the days of your life."

Genesis 3:14

The people erupted in a roar of disapproval and commotion. Some supported Cain and declared that Adam must be made the rightful king, while others shouted invectives and curses against Cain and said that they would never submit to the authority of another man. In the general chaos I could not make out who was on Adam's side and who wasn't. People were arguing with each other randomly while completely uninformed of each other's views. Several times Cain attempted to calm the crowd but they paid him no mind. The invocations of Abel and Seth were equally unsuccessful. Such was the violence of the crowd's unrest that I felt sure it was about to come to blows, when suddenly everyone froze, their eyes fixed upon the hill. An unutterable silence filled the meadow. The air was thick with an atmosphere of the crowd's shame and regret for its own insolence, for it had seen a sight that had made it mute with wonder. Standing on the hill above the crowd, where Cain had been just a moment before, was Adam.

Eve stood by Adam's side. She peered upon the crowd and caught my eye as Adam prepared to speak. Her gaze seemed to be filled with triumph and joy. The people expectantly waited to hear what Adam had to say.

Adam stood over the slaughtered serpent. He bent down and picked it up. To the crowd's astonishment and surprise, the serpent was once again in one piece. It raised its head towards Adam and hissed at the crowd. Adam turned to Eve and exchanged the serpent for an apple she was holding in her hand. He bit into the apple, looked thoughtfully at the crowd, and then began to speak.

Power and glory filled each word as Adam's voice reverberated through the meadow. The crowd stood rooted to the spot, taking in his speech. The people were filled with shame and remorse for having, even temporarily, questioned the authority of a man so evidently majestic and wise. They listened carefully to Adam's arguments as he lamented the state of grievous abasement into which Eden had fallen and reprimanded them for acting so shamefully in a land where all of their needs were provided and where they should have been able to live in a state of perfect contentment and bliss.

No one dared dispute Adam's authoritative and overpowering words. While some silently disagreed in their hearts, they maintained strict silence in the presence of so venerable a figure. When Adam's speech was nearly ended, Eve released the serpent and allowed it to slither into the crowd, which divided into two halves to allow the serpent to pass. Adam said that whoever did not wish to acknowledge his kingship could follow the serpent back to their homes, but that the rest could stay and join his army. He said that the establishment of his kingdom was inevitable, that those who stayed would fight for him and triumph in the establishment of a new society.

About half of the crowd stayed in the fragrant meadow. The rest turned around sadly and, their heads hanging low, walked slowly out of the meadow, past the river, and into the trees. Those who remained watched closely to see what Adam would do. Still munching on his apple, Adam descended the hill and walked among the crowd. He greeted every individual, encouraging him or her and inquiring about his or her health and happiness. Occasionally he would pick a man and ask him to follow him. After he had finished mingling with the crowd, he returned to the hill with twelve strongly-built and muscular men following him. These twelve, he announced, would be his personal bodyguard. As for the rest of the crowd, all of the men of fighting age would be enlisted in his army. He patiently communicated his plans to the crowd.

Eden had become a place of corruption, Adam said. He would lead the people out of Eden into a new land, where he would establish his kingdom and a new rule of law. The crowd would first follow him to that land, and then he would return to Eden with his army to bring the rest of the people out, by force if necessary. The crowd listened to his plan with a spirit of submission. It acknowledged him as a holy man possessed of supernatural power and wisdom, and it allowed him to lead it to whatever place he desired.

When Adam's speech was over, and the crowd was preparing to move, I found Seth.

"So your father's plan was a success," I said to him.

"Was there ever any doubt?" Seth replied.

Cain grinned at me with a look as if to say, "I told you so."

I walked with Adam and his sons, leading the crowd of thousands to its new home. We left the meadow and passed the rivers, following a valley winding through the hills for two days and two nights. Finally we came to a place covered in fields of wheat and corn, full of rivers and springs and grazed by herds of sheep and cattle. There were green meadows and hills and mountains in the distance. No one had ever been this far out of Eden before.

Adam addressed the people, and told them that this was where they would stop. The people spread out over the land, building fires and spreading tents to sleep in.

I stood with Cain, Abel and Seth as we examined our surroundings.

"There are plenty of cattle to keep us fed," Abel exclaimed.

"We can live well off the land and fields of wheat," Seth replied.

"There is much more that we can do with our lives here," Cain said. "We will have a freedom to gather and build a society that we did not have in the primitive land of Eden."

I approached Cain. "It has been many days since I have seen Sarah," I said. "I am anxious to get back to her and make sure that she is safe."

"We will return to Eden tomorrow," Cain replied, "my father's army behind us. You will find Sarah and Nava and convey them back safely to this spot, along with the rest of Eden."

"What of the people who do not want to come?" I asked.

"My father is expecting a resistance," Cain said. "Most of those who are set against his plans will gather their forces and attack us in a last-ditch attempt to maintain their autonomy. When we have defeated them, the rest will willingly come."

"We have over a thousand strong men, but we still may be outnumbered," I said.

"My father has promised that we will win an easy victory," Cain replied, nonchalantly.

That night, we fashioned spears out of the branches of trees and feasted in preparation for the next day. The men of Adam's army had separated from the rest of the people and were camped by themselves in a field. We had fires glowing and we talked late into the night before falling asleep beneath the low-hanging stars. The next day, Cain led the army back toward Eden. Abel and Seth walked with him. Adam stayed behind with Eve, tending to the rest of the people and awaiting the victorious return of his sons on the day when he would be crowned the new king.

I walked behind the sons of Adam, Heber by my side. We talked as the army made its way through the valley snaking between the hills as it approached the fragrant meadow between the two rivers and the forests of Eden.

"I'm not sure if we'll regret following Adam out of Eden like this," Heber said to me. He stepped carefully over the small rocks strewn across our path.

I dismissed his doubts. "The people of Eden know that Adam is the wisest of us all," I said. "Besides, I would not want my daughter growing up in the world we've left behind."

"I do not have a daughter," Heber said, "nor a wife."

"I think perhaps you will have both once Adam has established his kingdom," I replied.

"I prefer my freedom and the pursuit of pleasure," Heber said.

"I am not sure that you will have a choice, my friend," I said. "Adam intends to establish his law."

"If the people knew how strict Adam intends to be with his power, I am not sure he would have so many supporters," Heber said.

"The people trust him," I replied. "And they do so rightly. He will not lead them astray."

As we neared the place where Adam had given his speech, our scouts reported that a large army was waiting there. Cain stopped the march and addressed our men.

"Those who wish for Eden to remain as it has always been are making their last stand against us," he said. "We are fighting for honor, for progress, for the greatness of man. They fight for their right to remain sunk in degradation and shame. They want to be savages, but we want to be men. In the name of all that is good, we will crush them and not rest until every last one of them has been reduced to a pile of bones and flesh fallen upon the ground."

The men cheered, and we held our spears aloft as we walked over the last remaining hills between us and the army. When we came to the last hill, we looked down at the meadow and saw it covered with men. They had come from throughout Eden with one goal in mind: to oppose the will of Adam. The sons of Adam led the charge down the hill, shouting fiercely as they sprinted toward their opponents. The men we were fighting were armed with spears and clubs. I gripped a spear in each hand, running toward the approaching battle with Heber by my side.

Cain was the first one to join the fight. Sprinting ahead of his brothers and the rest of the men, he leaped headlong into a sea of clubs and spears, a hatchet in each hand, hacking wildly at those before him. The crowd parted as he entered into it and sent several men fiercely to their deaths. He was like a man possessed, and his enemies shrieked in wild excitement and fear. Abel and Seth entered close behind him, spears in hand, and came to the aid of their brother amidst a sea of enemies. They spilled the blood of many a man before the wall of men closed around them and they disappeared from sight.

Heber and I, and the rest of our army, joined the scene of the fight. I flung both spears at men in front of me who, pierced mortally, fell crashing to the ground. I stood over them and pulled out the spears, blood gushing out of the chest of one and the neck of the other. I screamed as I attacked a wall of men thrashing wildly at me with their fists and clubs. I received many blows but I inflicted more. Men fell before me as an invincible power seemed to flow through me. Beside me, I saw Heber standing victoriously over his foes. I do not know what ferocity possessed me, but I was oblivious of fatigue or pain. The routed enemy saw the fiery rage in my eyes and in those of my companions and they began to falter in their convictions. Momentarily paralyzed by surprise and fear, they watched helplessly as we stampeded over them and trampled them to the ground. Those who escaped this unexpected deluge turned tail to flee before us, but we did not let them go. We chased after them, overrunning them and striking them down as they ran. A sense of joyous exultation engulfed my soul. I chased the last remaining fighters into the trees of Eden, hurling spears at two of them from behind and finishing them off with a large wooden club I had picked up during the fight. A few remaining men scattered into the forest, and our fastest runners chased after them with the intent of leaving no man standing. I let them go. The battle was over, and we had won.

I found Heber standing over a fallen man, beating him to a pulp with his club. I put my hand on his shoulder. "The battle is over," I said.

He looked up at me, his face and hair matted with blood, wild rage in his eyes. Then his expression cleared, and he laughed. "That's it?" he said. He was incredulous. It was so easy.

"We have won the fight," I said.

"Do you think the sons of Adam made it?" I asked, scanning the men. I couldn't see Cain, Abel or Seth.

"I don't know," Heber replied.

I walked back toward the spot where I had seen them last. Sure enough, Cain was standing there, his arm around Abel, laughing. Seth was standing some way off, talking to the men. I took a deep breath.

Cain saw me, and greeted me warmly. "It is as my father had promised," he said. "We defeated our foes breezily. They hardly put up a fight."

"They should have known better than to oppose my father," Abel said.

I agreed. "Adam's wisdom and power is supernatural, and his cause is righteous. If it was not, how would we have been so strengthened as to defeat our enemies without the least resistance or trouble?"

11

To the woman He said: "I will greatly multiply your sorrow and your conception; in pain you shall bring forth children; your desire shall be for your husband, and he shall rule over you."

Genesis 3:16

As we in Adam's victorious army surveyed the wreckage of the battle we had just fought, we discovered that fewer than two hundred of our own men had died, while over two thousand of the men fighting against us had perished. We attributed such results to the supernatural power which Adam had and the authority he commanded over the hearts and minds of men, whether or not they recognized it. We felt assured that his assumption of the kingdom was correct and that we had done good, both for ourselves and for others, to fight for him.

After the battle I took leave of Heber and informed Cain, Abel and Seth that I would be departing their company.

"All of the men of this force are to be employed in rounding up the people of Eden and summoning them to Adam's presence in the land beyond the hills," Cain said.

"Unlike you all, I have a wife," I replied. "It is my duty to take care of her. I have to go find out what has happened to her, if she is alright; and when I find her, I intend to escort her back to our new land myself."

"Let him go," Seth said. "He has a responsibility to the girl, a responsibility that we have fought to protect."

Cain wanted to object, but Abel supported Seth's position. "His first duty is to his wife and daughter," he said.

Cain allowed me to go, so I went off by myself. I walked into the trees of Eden and found the path leading to my home. It would be a walk of three days, so I whistled as I walked. I thought of the battle and the victory which the supporters of Adam had just accomplished. Much blood had been shed, but the men who had died fighting us had been worthless, good for nothing, full of vice and foolishness. I trembled with rage to think of the fact that they had fought to preserve a world that would have been nothing but hell for my daughter. I would not want my daughter to live in the world I grew up in. It had been barbaric; I had been a barbarian. I couldn't imagine exposing her to such influences. At that moment I knew that Adam had saved my life and that of my family. Without him, I would not have even had a family. He had civilized me; he had brought me sanity. He had made me a man.

I had a good heart; that is what Sarah always said. If only she knew me as I was before. She had known me as I was before. Why didn't she recognize who I had been? I had no morals. I cared only for myself. I killed her family because I cared only for myself. She didn't see that. All she saw was my heart, that it had been good. And maybe it was. Maybe my heart was good. Maybe I had always wanted to do right. I just didn't know what that meant. I didn't know how to be the man I was supposed to be. Adam helped me see it. He taught and educated me. And he didn't do it through words, he did it through his spirit. Just by being with me, by thinking of me, by standing firm and not budging when I didn't want to be with Sarah. By swooping in and rescuing me from my own abyss of heedlessness. He had truly saved my life.

Where would I be without him? Would I be one of those dead on the battlefield now, fighting for neither cause nor value? Or would I be like Heber, fighting on the side of right merely because I had nothing else to do? It didn't matter now, I had something else to do. I had a family to care for. I wouldn't disappoint them.

With each step I thanked Adam, and felt grateful that I had been born during his lifetime. Had I been born a generation earlier, I wouldn't have had Nava to love and care for. I wouldn't have known how to be a father. I wouldn't have known the pleasure and comfort of having a wife.

I didn't miss the wild life. I didn't miss its pleasures. I had been dead, now I was alive. I had been in prison, now I was set free. I had been an animal, now I was a man. A dignified man, a man with honor, a man with values, a purpose and a destiny. A man with a wife who loved him and a daughter who needed him. A beautiful wife, and a beautiful daughter, both of whom I dearly cherished.

I found Sarah sitting by the fire, Nava in her arms. The baby was asleep. I walked quietly toward the clearing where she sat.

"Sarah," I said.

She looked up, joy and hope in her eyes.

"Emmanuel!" she exclaimed.

The baby awoke as Sarah got up and ran towards me. I opened my arms and held both my wife and daughter in my embrace.

Sarah giggled. "You're beard's grown long!" she said.

I laughed. "I'll have to shave it while I'm here," I said. "Afterward, we're leaving, and we're not coming back."

"I heard the men of Eden were preparing for a big fight," Sarah said. "I was so worried that you would be hurt."

I looked at her seriously. "There was a battle, between those who fought for Adam and those who wanted things to stay as they were. Adam's army won."

"So you were successful," she said. "Where's Cain?"

"The sons of Adam and their men are taking the people of Eden to a land beyond the hills where Adam is establishing his kingdom," I replied. "I departed from them in order to find you and escort you back safely myself."

Nava yawned and blinked at me several times, then gave me the most beautiful smile I had ever seen. She leaned away from her mother and reached out her arms toward me. I took her from her mother and cradled her lovingly, rocking her back and forth. Love gushed out from my heart as I saw a piece of myself and of Sarah reflected before me.

"She's so beautiful," I said, "and she's grown in the month I was gone."

"She can crawl now," Sarah said, "and she said her first word yesterday."

I looked at Sarah, astonished. "Oh really?" I said. "What did she say?"

"Daddy," Sarah said, with a laugh.

"Daddy?" I said, surprised. "The first word she said was my name?"

"When you were gone, I used to hold Nava in my arms and tell her about you. About how good and faithful you are, and how you are coming back to us. And you're here now."

"And did she understand you?" I asked. "I mean, did she know that 'daddy' is me?"

"I don't know," Sarah said. "Ask her yourself."

I looked at Nava, and tickled her chin. "Do you know that your daddy is me?" I asked.

She just laughed up at me, her wide eyes fixed on mine.

"I think she knows," Sarah said.

I held Sarah's hand and gave her a kiss on her lips. "Thank you for waiting for me," I said.

"Duty called," Sarah said. "Eden needed you. I understand you, Emmanuel. I'll never keep you from doing what you have to do."

"You know, I'm the luckiest man in the world to have you," I said.

"And you know," Sarah said, leaning towards me. "You're the best man I've ever had," she said.

"You mean…" I said.

"Yes," she said. "During sex."

I smiled, and looked at Nava. I was quite satisfied with myself. "And this is the product of our love," I said. "Isn't she amazing?"

"She is the most beautiful child I have ever seen," Sarah said. "I am going to need you to protect her, Emmanuel."

"That's what I'm here for," I said.

Sarah put her arm around my waist. "Don't ever leave my side," she said.

"I won't," I said.

"Sarah," I said.

"What?" she asked.

"I've… I've been away a long time."

Sarah smiled. "After she's asleep."

"Isn't she tired?" I asked.

"I think so," Sarah said. "I'll put her to bed."

Sarah went inside the hut as I sat by the fire. I wanted the girl. Every time I saw her I wanted her more. She just grew on me every day, every time we made love. I couldn't have enough of her. I would never have enough.

When Sarah came out of the hut, she was naked. I gasped and caught my breath. She was stunning.

"Sarah," I said.

"Shhh…" she said. She was wearing black eyeliner, which made her very seductive.

I took my shirt off and then dropped my loincloth. My six-pack flexed as my abdomen clenched in desire, I wanted her so much. She looked at my muscular chest, and then lowered her gaze.

"I can see you want me," she said.

"I want to ravish you and protect you at the same time," I said. "I've never felt so conflicted."

"You can do both," Sarah said.

We made love for hours until the moon came out in the sky. Sarah and I lay side by side under the stars. "You know, it's been a long time since I've eaten," I said.

"How long?" Sarah asked.

"A day, maybe more."

We ate figs and peaches that Sarah had gathered that morning.

"It's late," Sarah said.

We went inside the hut, where the child was sleeping. I took Sarah in my arms and we lay down beside Nava, falling asleep to the sound of her tiny breath.

The next morning we left our home for the final time. We didn't take anything with us, just the clothes on our backs. Everything we needed on the way would be provided. And where we were going, we would start over from scratch. I had high hopes for a new life in Adam's kingdom, the first kingdom the world had ever known. It would be a good place to raise my daughter.

We took turns carrying Nava. I would have carried her the whole time but Sarah liked doing so. I told Sarah about the beautiful life that Nava would have, and how many precious brothers and sisters she would have, as she grew up.

"Last night was too good," Sarah said. "I wouldn't be surprised if another baby is on the way."

"I hope it's a son," I said.

Sarah looked surprised. "You don't want another daughter?" she asked.

"It's not like that," I said. "I would love another daughter. It's just that I want Nava to have a brother who will protect her from the other boys."

Sarah laughed. "You will be there as well, Emmanuel," she said.
I frowned. "I might not always be here, Sarah," I said. "I need to know that you and Nava will be protected."

"We have the sons of Adam to take care of that," Sarah said. "They like us. Remember?"

Because of these words of Sarah, I felt reassured. She was right. Cain, Abel and Seth were good friends, and Sarah and I had been the first to follow their father's teachings. They would take care of Sarah and Nava if I was gone.

"But nothing will happen to you," Sarah said.

"I'll do everything in my power to be here, and remain here, as long as you two need me," I said.

When we left the trees of Eden, we saw that the men who had been killed in the battle were still lying there, rotting. I guided Sarah around the battlefield, pointing out the place where Cain and Adam had made their speeches. Then we walked through the valley between the hills, finally making it to where the people of Eden had been encamped a couple of days later. Cain, Abel, Seth and the men of Adam's army hadn't come back yet. The old men, the women and the children who were loyal to Adam were there waiting, however. Some of the people in the camp recognized me, and they went and informed Adam that we had arrived. He came out to greet us himself. I cannot describe the warmth, graciousness and generosity he displayed on that occasion. He gifted me with a spear tipped with a stone blade that he himself had carved, and said with a laugh that I could use it to protect my daughter, which he knew was what I wanted to do above all else. He also greeted Sarah and thanked her for putting up with me, which made me laugh. He then took Nava in his arms, and she instantly took a liking to him. When Adam wanted to hand her back to me, she didn't want to come. He lovingly told her that I was her father, and that I would take care of her better than anyone else could. She didn't understand him, but she seemed calmed by his words. She came to me, squeezing me tightly by the neck with her tiny arms.

Eve came out to greet us as well, and gave Sarah a bearskin gown that she herself had made. Seth had killed the bear, Eve said proudly. Adam and Eve seemed especially to love their youngest son. I didn't know why, but they seemed to cherish him for reasons I could not understand, as if they knew what wonderful things lay in his future.

Even though Eve was old enough to be Sarah's mother, it was clear why people said she was the most beautiful woman in the world. When Adam guessed my thoughts, he told me that when he had first lay eyes on Eve, he decided right then and there that a man should have one woman, and one woman only. He had also understood that a man could not properly care for a woman unless he was hers alone. I marveled at the love the two so evidently shared, the warmth that flowed between them like electricity easily felt by all those who stood in their presence. When Eve looked at Adam, she did so with so much respect and admiration. It was clear that she loved him, and I knew that the only way a man could attract such unbridled devotion was if he loved a woman with all his heart, and showed her that love every day in deeds as well as in words. I only hoped that Sarah and I could live up to the model of fellowship and love that Adam and Eve so strikingly displayed.

12

Then to Adam He said, "Because you have heeded the voice of your wife, and have eaten from the tree of life which I commanded you, saying, 'You shall not eat of it': Cursed is the ground for your sake; in toil you shall eat of it all the days of your life. Both thorns and thistles it shall bring forth for you, and you shall eat the herb of the field. In the sweat of your face you shall eat bread till you return to the ground, for out of it you were taken; for dust you are, and to dust you shall return."

Genesis 3:17-19

Adam graciously invited Sara, Nava and I to stay in a tent set up next to his and Eve's. I gratefully complied. It was an honor to be considered so highly by Adam, but it was also a delight to be near him and spend time with him. He was a constant source of comfort, reassurance, and hope, which I strove to share with Sara and my daughter.

The next day, the first group of men returned from Eden, with a large company of woman and children following them. We set them up in tents erected throughout the plain. When everybody arrived, there would be more than ten thousand men, women and children ready to start a new life in a new land. Under Adam's guidance, I led a large group of the newly arrived men out into the plain to hunt the buffalo that were roaming in large herds outside our camp. We would use their skins to build new tents for the people who would be arriving soon, and their meat for food.

My old friend Caleb was among the men who went out with me to hunt the buffalo. The first herd we found was roaming just outside the camp. We advanced quietly toward them, wooden spears in each hand. They didn't even notice us as they grazed on the wild-growing wheat and grass. Caleb noticed that a lot of wheat and other grains were growing in the new land we occupied.

"Adam says that it can be used for food," I said. "He said that later, when everything is in place, he will show us all how to cook it. He says it needs to be crushed."

"Interesting," Caleb said. "But right now I'm in a mind for some buffalo."

He ran toward the herd, a spear in each hand, and cast them both into the side of the buffalo grazing nearest to him. It groaned loudly and fell over on its side, the rest of the herd scattering away in fear. I caught up with Caleb after a sprint which left me breathing heavily.

"Why did you go and do that?" I asked. "Now you've scared off the herd."

"Animals were never scared off in Eden, no matter what we did to them," Caleb replied, confused.

"We're not in Eden anymore," I said. "Or did you not get the memo?"

"No, I didn't. I didn't know things would be so different here," Caleb said.

"We'll they are, so you'll have to get used to it. Things aren't just going to be handed to us on a silver platter. We have to work for things now. Remember, that's what Adam wanted us to have: responsibility."

Caleb sighed. "I guess I'll just follow your lead."

"That's a good idea."

The rest of the men had caught up to us. The oldest and wisest of them, Kesad, pulled the spears out of the fallen buffalo and handed them back to Caleb. He pointed at the herd, which had stopped to graze again only several hundred yards away.

"We walk quietly amongst the herd, and then each of us casts our spears into a different buffalo at the same time," he said. "Then we drag them back to the camp."

"We'll wait until more men have come to drag the meat back to the camp," I said. "For now, we will skin the buffalo where they are and bring the hides back to the camp to build tents."

Each of us had with us a razor-sharp stone, used as a knife, to cut away the buffalo skins from their flesh.

"Off we go, then," Caleb said. He whistled happily as we walked toward the buffalo.

"Quiet," I said.

"Sorry."

We made it to the herd of buffalo, and quietly walked amongst them. Again, they didn't notice us.

"These things don't learn very fast," Caleb said.

But his voice alarmed the herd, and the buffalo began to scatter.

"Attack!" I yelled.

Each of the men immediately sunk his spears into one of the buffalo. I stabbed both of mine into a buffalo's neck. It fell on its knees before me, blood squirting out of its neck all over my legs.

"Sorry," I whispered. I removed the spears and cast one into its heart, killing it instantly.

The rest of the men experienced similar success. We got to work with the hides. The cutting was methodical. We cut the skin just under the neck, then down across the belly all the way to the tail. From that cut we made four additional cuts, one down each leg, and from those initial cuts we pulled the skin and stretched it off the carcasses. In this way, we ended up with whole buffalo hides, only two of which would be enough to make a tent.

We repeated the process all day, and made it back to the camp that night with over a hundred buffalo hides. More people had arrived, among them Heber and Seth.

I first found Seth. He greeted me, and told me that Abel and Cain had gone the deepest into Eden, to the very depths of it, rounding up everybody they could find. He said they would be back tomorrow.

"You must be anxious to see your parents," I said, "and I am sure they are waiting for you."

He smiled, put his hand on my shoulder, and began to walk toward his parents' tent.

I then found Heber. He was with the girl from the forest, the exceedingly beautiful one who had tried to seduce me when I had first started life with Sarah. She smiled at me mischievously when I greeted them. I smiled back.

"I see you've managed to catch someone in your net," I told her. Heber laughed. "It's obvious that Adam's going to make us each choose one," he said. "So I'm not going to waste any time taking the most beautiful."

"I don't get chosen," the girl said. "I do the choosing."

"You've made a good choice," I replied. "Heber's a good man, and the best friend I have."

"I know," the girl said. "Before you, Emmanuel, no man had ever rejected me. It impressed me that you were so good to Sarah. So I wanted to know who your friends were. It didn't surprise me that Heber was a good man too."

"I have to admit, you made me think twice," I said. "But once again, Adam intervened in my life, and gave me the courage to stay true to Sarah, and to myself."

"Adam has done well for all of us," Heber said. "There's something good about choosing a single partner, isn't there?"

"Something wholesome," the girl agreed.

"What's your name, anyway?" I asked.

"Ada," she said.

"Isn't she beautiful?" Heber asked. "Even more beautiful than Eve, if you ask me."

"That's what I think about Sarah," I said.

"Nobody is as beautiful as Eve," Sarah said. I turned around to see her standing there with Eve by her side. Eve was holding Nava in her arms.

Technically speaking, Sarah was right. Eve's beauty was unequalled, even though she was over forty. Still, I felt Sarah had a charm all her own.

"It's hard to reason with a man when he's in love," I smiled.

"And who is this wonderful creature?" Eve asked, extending a hand to Ada.

"Ada," the girl replied, taking Eve's hand and blushing slightly.

"Adam told me to expect you tonight," Eve said. "He said you were the second girl in Eden to find a man."

"Third, actually," Ada replied. "You were the first."

Eve laughed. "Well, I guess you're right. And so you've fallen for Emmanuel's friend?"

"We've fought passionately, in the name of bachelorhood, many a time side by side," Heber said. I laughed. Sara gave me a look.

"Those days are over, Heber," Ada said.

"I know, dearest," Heber said, taking her into his arms. "And I don't regret that."

"You'd better not," Sarah said.

"Adam wants such commitments to become official," Eve said. "He wants marriage to become a way of life for every man and woman. So he wants the four of you, Eden's first two couples, to swear fealty to each other in a public ceremony this very night. If you will, I will lead you to him."

Sarah looked at me happily. "Isn't that great?" she asked. "Very nice," I assured her, taking her hand. Heber and Ada fell in line behind us, and we followed Eve to the front of a gathering crowd, where Adam was standing. He was preparing to speak. Adam received us warmly. He greeted us, warmly embraced Heber and Ada, and said that they were very welcome. Just then, a commotion rose up throughout the crowd. Cain and Abel had returned, and with them were thousands of men, women and children—the rest of the people of Eden.

Cain told the people with him to mix in with the crowd which was already there and he came forward with Abel by his side. Adam greeted them lovingly and heard their report about what had transpired since they left. Then Adam raised his hand, and the crowd became quiet. A moment later, Adam began to speak.

Adam greeted the people and told them that they were very welcome and very loved. Eden had become corrupt place, he said, a place of destruction and death no longer conduce to the best interests of human life. The people of Eden had lived in ignorance since the beginning of time, he said, and that had always been okay because no one knew better. But now people knew better, he said. Adam said that a time had come when people could tell the difference between right and wrong in their hearts. Deep inside, he said, everyone now knew that having unbridled sex, viewing the other sex as only the object of lust and passion, was wrong. People knew that selfishness, fighting and killing each other were wrong. People knew that love and fidelity, courage and responsibility, were valuable. And if they didn't know, Adam said, he was teaching them these things now. The people of Eden had come to a point of no return, a point where they had to accept the difference between good and evil and act accordingly. They had to make a choice—they could either choose to live their lives for the sake of passion, or they could have a passion for the purpose of their lives. Because they were here now, Adam said, they had chosen purpose over passion. It should be acceptable to them, therefore, Adam said, that now there would be a law, to help people remember and value the difference between right and wrong. Wrong acts would be condemned and punished, and righteous acts would be valued and rewarded. A gasp went through the crowd as Adam said this, but no one objected, so Adam continued. There would be three laws in the new society, Adam said. First, there would be no killing. Second, there would be no stealing. Third, everyone would have to get married, and they would only be allowed to have sex with their partner. A stir went through the crowd, and Adam continued. If people chose to remain single, he said, they could not have sex with anyone. A few people murmured complaints upon hearing this, so Adam continued to speak about the values he wanted the people of Eden to exemplify. At present, he said, the people of Eden did not know the meaning of the word 'love'. This was because they were living like animals. But love, Adam said, was the only thing that could make anyone, the people of Eden included, truly happy. Without love, life would cease entirely. Adam did not want the people to destroy themselves. He wanted them to thrive, to be content and to prosper. Because of this, he said, people had to learn to act in ways that fostered love. They had to learn to live by rules and regulations that enabled love to grow among them. Uninhibited sex with anyone, he said, was making love into a cheap commodity. But that shouldn't be the case. Love should be highly cherished and very valuable. In the same way, a man and a woman must cherish and value each other. The only way to do this was to be good, faithful and loyal to another individual, to love them and to promise to love them alone for the rest of one's life. The benefit of such a lifestyle, Adam said, was inestimable. People themselves would realize how much better life is once they have firm commitments in place. No one denied this. Through many such exhortations and kindly arguments, Adam succeeded in subduing the people and convincing them that his rule of law was in their best interests. By the end of his talk, they gladly agreed to comply with all of the specifications Adam had set in place. They also unanimously arose and told Adam that they wanted him to be their king. Because of this, Adam gratefully proclaimed that he would be the first king of Eden, and that he would take upon himself the responsibility of ensuring Eden's well-being, and that people followed the laws of morality that he had set in place. The punishments for breaking the laws, he said, would be decided by him on a case by case basis, but he promised to always be just in his judgments. No one doubted him—Adam was the wisest, most just and trustworthy man they had ever known. And thus, Adam became Eden's first king, and Eden had its first kingdom. Most significantly, at the end of his talk, Adam said that he would be renaming the land they lived in. While before all had lived in Eden, Adam said, now their home would be called Earth. Adam, Eve and their sons would lead the people in their new life on Earth, and make sure that everyone thrived and was well cared for.

The last thing Adam did that night was to announce that besides Eve and himself, Earth had its first two couples, and he wanted to marry them officially in a public ceremony to be witnessed by all. He then asked Sarah and me to step forward. We stepped to the front of the crowd, where we were greeted by Eve. She took Nava from Sara, gave us garlands of roses and asked us to stand facing each other, holding each other's hands. I smiled and gazed into Sarah's eyes as Adam performed his benediction. He spoke of the meaning of marriage and its importance, and then he joked that it had taken an army and a war to help me realize what a gem I had in the girl standing before me, but that I had finally come around. And he said that Sarah was a model for how a woman in marriage should be, having full and unbridled devotion to a man. I held Sarah in my arms, gave her a kiss, and we were married.

Everybody cheered. Afterward, Adam and Eve repeated the process with Heber and Ada, and then Cain spoke and helped everybody with the logistics of where they would be eating and sleeping that night. Adam had appointed a large number of men to make a feast of buffalo meat for everybody on Earth, and we celebrated the first day of our new lives, eating and talking long into the night before going into our tents or sleeping out under the open sky.

13

Then the Lord God said, "Behold, the man has become like one of Us, to know good and evil. And now, lest he put out his hand and take also of the tree of life, and eat, and live forever"—therefore the Lord God sent him out of the garden of Eden to till the ground from which he was taken.

Genesis 2:22-23

Men started thinking about what women they wanted to marry. Women started doing likewise. When asked for his plans for the community's life on Earth, Adam replied that he would not make any decisions until all of the people were married. People set to work, then, getting to know each other and making their choices. For most people, however, there wasn't that much to know. Many people were already familiar with each other. Their sense of who they wanted to marry, also, wasn't very sophisticated either. People didn't think too much or too hard about it. Mostly they just thought about who was most attractive to them. Many had already slept with each other before, and were familiar with who piqued their interests. The first day after Sarah and I were married, a number of the most attractive men and women chose each other and informed Adam that they wanted to be married. Adam married these couples together that night. There were others, also, who just knew who the person for them was. These people made their decisions quickly and decisively. Following their example, the rest of the people followed suit.

Most people didn't want to go too long without having sex, so they just chose someone and got it over with. Adam married off hundreds of couples in the first few days. For the first people of Earth, there weren't concepts of love and deep friendship for them to consider before marriage. All they had known of the opposite sex before related to them being objects of lust and passion, and they initially took marriage to be a mutual contract of sexual satisfaction. Adam knew that the relationships would evolve from this sorry starting point, however. Through the challenges and tests of marriage which he knew would come, people would learn the principles of commitment and dedication, and through mutual struggles and growth they would eventually come to love and deeply respect each other. The first people of Earth weren't a picky or demanding people. They didn't expect too much of each other. Like I said, they were easy going. Marriage for them, in those early years, wasn't something difficult.

Some people, bereft of an idea of their own, begged Adam to choose a partner for them. Adam graciously hand-picked many such matches. Inevitably, these marriages turned out to be the best and most successful. Not that any marriages were blatantly unsuccessful; we didn't have such a thing as divorce. When people married that first time, they were stuck with their partners for the rest of their lives. People were not grieved by this eventuality, however. They soon found that the challenges of life outside of Eden were greater than any they had known before. They would have to work hard to survive and thrive, and their partners in marriage became their greatest source of strength and support. The newlywed couples would come to rely on each other and depend on each other with a real, continued need. For most of them, life without the other would eventually become unthinkable.

Most of the new couples had a lot of fun with each other. The new adventure they were embarking on, with such an admired and capable leader as Adam at the helm, held a new fascination and delight for each of them, and invigorated their fledgling unions. People took pleasure in the arms and laps of partners who would be theirs, Adam promised, for all eternity. The people of those early years weren't weak or frail. They were strong, healthy, and nearly all attractive. The individuals comprising the first marriages led robust and pleasurable sex lives. The sounds of lovemaking could be heard heavily coming from tents throughout the camp deep into every night. Those people who had not married yet were impelled by this thick atmosphere dripping with love and desire to make their choices so that they, too, could join in the fun of the world's first unions. The sex, with a soul-mate and committed partner, people eagerly reported to their friends and acquaintances, was much better than it had ever been in the wanton and passion-filled orgies of Eden. There was passion in the new marriages, indeed, but it was a passion tempered with an intangible spirit of connectedness and spiritual desire which Adam called love.

After a fortnight, everybody in the camp was married. Adam was well-pleased with the spirit of obedience to his teaching that everybody evinced in doing this, and he spoke to us of the benefits and goodness which would accrue to us on account of our making these commitments. Sarah and I just looked at each other and smiled. What had seemed impossible just a few months before had become a reality. The people of Eden had heeded Adam's commands and reformed their conduct. What had been a world of disorder and chaos had become one of discipline and accountability. Nor had there been so much as a fight between anyone since the day the people of Eden had arrived in the camp. Adam's constant advice and admonitions that the people of Earth should live together in peace had irradiated the spirit of the people with cooperation and unity. People went out of their way to help each other and were concerned with each other's affairs. All wished each other well and did their utmost to ensure that no one experienced sadness or discomfort. So great a transformation in the character and conduct of the people was a source of great amazement to both myself and others who were possessed of understanding and wisdom. We marveled at how Adam had, single-handedly and alone, turned a race of barbarians and savages into a budding civilization that promised to reflect a paradise of which the delights of Eden had been only a fading and poorly sustained image. I looked with satisfaction upon the initial stages of a society that would be the habitation of my daughter Nava for the rest of her newly begun life on Earth. I reflected with gratitude that it would be one of peace and security, a home of order and moral integrity. No longer would she face the prospect of a childhood in a garden which was really a wasteland of corruption. Salvation, I was assured, had been accomplished for my children and for theirs as well.

Adam let the people settle into their new lives for several weeks after they had been married. During that time, we lived off of buffalo, sheep and oxen that wandered in herds around the plains, and Adam had introduced a method of grinding the wild-growing grains into flour that was mixed with water and baked to produce a new and nutritious food called bread. There were many fields of such grains growing in the new land we inhabited.

Twenty days after the last marriage had been contracted, Adam again addressed the people. He commended them for their efforts and exhorted them to mutual love, cooperation and commitment in their relationships. He then announced the plans for life after Eden. The people of Earth, he said, would live in communities defined by trust and cooperation. Each one of his sons would found a community according to his desire and interest. The people would be free to choose which of these communities they wished to join, but life as individuals free from an overarching society, Adam stated, was over.

After Adam had finished giving his address, Seth spoke to the people. We all turned to him reverently and listened to his words with great interest.

"Dearly loved people of Earth," Seth said. "Life as we know it has changed forever. Gone are the days when we were free of responsibility and accountability. Gone are the days when we had no moral compass, no set of values to guide our thoughts, words and actions. Now we are a changed people. We have become enlightened and matured. We know the meaning of goodness; we appreciate the value of morality. Adam has educated us to such a degree that we hate vice and conflict. We have a spirit of fellowship and good-feeling for each other and we are committed to working together to build a new life in a new land. I want to found a community that values the spirit of grace and moral integrity that my father, Adam, has brought us. There are many grains and nutritious plants growing in this land. I will teach you how to take the seeds of these plants and sow them in rich soil, creating farms off of which we can live prosperously for the rest of our lives. Each married couple will have their own plot of land and their own farm, and they will raise their children together in these new homes. Other families will be working alongside them and will provide them with any needed assistance and support. As a community, we will value joy and pleasure, but we will also strive to know contentment, moderation, and peace. We will value character above all else and we will grow both personally and as a community so that our children, and our children's children after us, can live even better lives than we do now. I hope that you will join me in this new community."

The people cheered Seth, and he stepped aside and let Abel speak. "Dear people of Eden," Abel said. "You all know the importance of the land. It provides us with all of our needs. Nature is our guide, our protector, our helper and our support. In Eden, the natural world gave us all that we had. We never lacked anything; all was provided. In the new land we inhabit, I want us to continue to value our relationship with nature. Without the land and the sky, without water and air and earth and fire, without the animals and plants that surround us, we could not live or be able to survive. There are herds of buffalo, bison, cattle, sheep, goats, oxen, and other livestock wandering in great numbers throughout this land. We can live as herders and keepers of these animals, living off of their flesh and milk and allowing them to supply all of our needs. We will have respect for these animals, and we will appreciate the sustenance they give us. Our community will live in harmony with each other and with the world around us. We will be friends to ourselves first, to our neighbors second and to nature third. Trust and cooperation will define our new society. I believe that we can live simply and freely. Life on Earth does not have to be complicated. We can learn much from each other and from the world around us. We can live, grow and thrive in a world that we know as sacred because it is our home. I hope you will join me in the community that I will found."

Even more people cheered Abel's speech, and then Cain stood in front of the people and spoke. "Dearly loved and highly respected people of Earth," Cain said. "You all know what my father has done to us. We were little better than animals; he has taught us to be men. We were base, immoral and degraded; Adam has improved us, raised us up, inspired us, educated us, taught us wisdom, given us knowledge, imparted to us discipline, and gathered us into a new life in a real society. I want this society to advance and grow. I do not want us to go back in the direction of the ways from which we came. We lived off the land in Eden, but now I want us to become the masters of the land on Earth. We are greater than nature, because we possess intelligence and intellect and nature does not. We must use our intellects to advance and make life ever easier for ourselves. I want to found a city in which we will work together to live above the world of nature. We can know rest and ease and we can become civilized and sophisticated. We can continue to enjoy the pleasures and happiness of life while knowing the greatness of dominion and mastery over it. I want us to use our minds and our thoughts to seize control from the world around us. If you join my community, you will be joining the greatest and highest community on Earth. We will live with moral values, yes, but we will also advance along physical and material lines. The glories of the city I will found will be better than anything you have ever experienced in Eden or will experience in the communities founded by my brothers, Abel and Seth. Together we will discover the secrets of nature and will invent ways and means by which we can become invincible and indestructible. Abel says we can live simply, but I say that we can find sophistication. Adam has already separated us from the animals; why stop where we are? Let us keep going, keep advancing and improving. In the city, each of us will specialize in a unique trade or job, and by this means we will found a society possessing complexity, full of entertainment and delight. We will found new technologies that will, through the genius of human innovation, indeed make life simple and easy for all of us. I invite you all to join my new community in the cities."

Cain's speech received the loudest applause of all. After Cain spoke, Adam returned to his place before the people and told them that these three communities would commence life on Earth. Adam and Eve themselves would live outside these communities as the first rulers and authority on Earth, and would oversee the affairs of all of the people. They would enforce justice and guide the fledgling communities in their affairs. The rest of the people, they said, would now be obligated to decide which of their sons they wished to follow in the days ahead. The people would have three weeks to make their choice. For three more weeks, the people would remain united in the camp. After that time, they would break off into their new groups, and begin their new lives. Life on Earth wouldn't be as easy or as effortless as it was in Eden, Adam emphasized. By giving the people these three options, he hoped that everyone could choose the new lifestyle that best suited them and their interests.

14

Now Adam knew Eve his wife, and she conceived and bore Cain, and said, "I have acquired a man from the Lord."

Genesis 4:1

That night, Sarah and I discussed which of the new communities we wanted to join. We had already eaten dinner and Nava had gone to sleep. We were sitting together in our tent, looking into each other's eyes and debating the merits of each community.

"Seth's seems like the best to me, Emmanuel," Sarah said. "He emphasizes character and the meeting of responsibility. I just feel the most comfortable about his plan."

"Seth is good, no doubt," I replied, "but then again, they all are. I like Cain's idea about progress and advancement. I really want Nava to live a good and comfortable life. She will have more opportunities in the city Cain plans."

"I don't know about the city, Emmanuel," Sarah said. "We've lived in nature all our lives. What about Abel? He wants to respect nature and live in harmony with it."

"I'd rather live in Abel's community than Seth's," I said, "because herding cattle and sheep will be much easier than farming. I want to have my time to spend with you and the children, Sarah. I don't want to have to work out in the fields all day."

"Is that why you don't want to follow Seth?" Sarah asked. "Because you don't want to farm?"

"It's not that I don't want to work, Sarah," I said. "But I think there is more to life than hard work. We'll have it easier in Cain's city. I don't want to miss Nava's life as she grows up."

"I don't know about Cain, Emmanuel," Sarah said. She looked at me with wide eyes. "Remember when he wrestled you that first day by the river? He almost killed you, remember? He has a quick temper. He's unpredictable. I don't know if you can trust him."

"He didn't kill me, Sarah," I said. "And I was the one who challenged him to a wrestling match. He's been much different since then. We're good friends now. And he's Adam's eldest son. I don't think we can go wrong with him."

Sarah held my hands and sighed. "It's your choice, Emmanuel," Sarah said. "Wherever you want to go, I'll follow you. But I just hope you know what you're doing."

"Trust me, Sarah," I said. "We'll be fine. And if we don't like it in the city, we can always move. It's not like Cain is going to enslave us."

"I know he won't," Sarah said.

I smiled and drew my finger across Sarah's cheek. "You're precious to me, Sarah. I'll protect you. I promise that whatever happens, you and Nava will be alright."

Sarah took my hand and kissed it. Then she drew it forward and pressed it to her heart. "I know, Emmanuel," she said.

"Here, come give me a hug," I said. I took Sarah into my arms and she nestled against my chest. I held her tight and squeezed. "You'll be safe," I said. She looked up at me with tender eyes, and I stroked her hair. Then she lifted her chin and we kissed, long and slow. I felt my pulse quicken and Sarah's skin heat up. "Let's make love," I said.

In the morning I took Nava in one arm, held Sarah's in another and walked out of my tent into the early dawn light. The air was fragrant with spices as roast bison had been cooking throughout the night. A number of men and women had baked large quantities of bread and were handing them out, along with vegetable and bison soup, at locations throughout the camp. People were out and about, stretching, chatting and getting ready for the day. There was an air of excitement as people discussed their choices for which community they wanted to live in.

I took a loaf of bread and handed it to Sara, and then I ladled two bowls of soup for myself and Sara. We sat down on a log beside a fire and ate as other people walked around us or sat down on logs to eat themselves. I broke the bread and handed some to Sarah. She had already breastfed Nava earlier that morning. Nava was eight months old now. She could crawl and say short sentences, like "I love mommy and daddy." She was a really smart child.

I took a bite of the bread and washed it down with a spoonful of soup. "This is good," I told Sarah.

"I could make it better," Sarah said.

I smiled. "I know you could."

"Good morning, Emmanuel, Sarah." It was Heber, with Ada by his side. They had brought their own bread and bowls of soup and sat down beside us.

"We had quite a discussion last night," Ada said to Sara. "We couldn't decide which of the brothers' communities to join."

"Oh, Emmanuel and I decided quite easily," Sarah said. I winked at her.

"Ada wanted to follow Cain, but I really liked what Seth said," Heber said. He sighed. "People don't understand Seth. If only they knew how valuable he is, they would all follow him."

"They're all the sons of Adam," I said. "None of them will lead us astray."

"I would have enjoyed life in the city," Ada said.

"So you chose Seth's farming community?" Sarah asked.

"No," Ada replied.

"We made a compromise," Heber said. "We chose Abel."

"How does that work?" I asked. "You wanted Seth and she wanted Cain, so you chose Abel?"

Heber laughed. I raised my eyebrow.

"I know neither of us got what we wanted," Heber said. "But that was kind of the point."

"We're both pretty stubborn," Ada sighed. "And neither of us wanted to budge."

"But then we made love," Heber said. "And we both wanted to please the other."

I looked at Sarah. I knew we were both thinking about the night before. She smiled sweetly.

"So then I said I wanted to go to Seth's community, and Heber said he wanted to go to the city," Ada said. "Then Heber suggested we just become herders with Abel. It seemed alright, so I agreed and we made love some more."

"That doesn't make any sense at all," I said.

Sarah shook her head. Heber gave Ada a kiss.

"I chose a good man," Ada said. "He knows how to make me happy."

Heber rolled his eyes. I laughed.

"Heber and I are both lucky men," I said.

"Real lucky," Heber said. Ada punched him on the arm. Heber picked her up and carried her back to their tent.

"Newlyweds," Sara said.

"Newlyweds," Nava repeated.

I laughed, and took Nava from Sarah. She laughed with me as I held her.

"You're the smartest little girl, you know that?" I said. I tickled her and the baby laughed some more.

"It never gets old, does it?" Sarah asked.

"What, marriage?" I said.

"Yeah," Sarah said thoughtfully.

"I don't know about others," I replied, "But I'm crazier about you now than the day I met you."

"You weren't crazy about me at all when you met me," Sarah said.
"I was very attracted to you, in fact," I replied matter-of-factly. "If I recall, I kept you longer than any other girl, no matter how pretty. I couldn't have enough of you."

"We didn't know what love was back then," Sarah reminisced. "But I knew you were different."

"How was I different?" I asked.

"You were the one for me," Sarah replied.

I looked at Nava. "And this is the child that sealed our bond," I said. Then I sighed and felt a dead weight in my chest as I thought about the fight I had with Morag and his relatives and friends.

"Look, Sarah," I said. "I've never really apologized to you about what happened with your family. But I'm starting to understand now how wrong I was. I know that's just how we acted in those days, but it still shouldn't have taken me so long to realize what I had in you. If only I had known how much you would mean to me one day, I would never have resisted starting a life with you."

Sarah looked at me compassionately. "You did well, Emmanuel. It wasn't your fault. You know that. And you know that I have no hard feelings about my family. You're my family now. And in fact, I'm glad you won that fight. I wouldn't want to have to live my life without you."

I kept staring at the ground. I felt so guilty. Sarah put down her plate and sat closer to me. "Look, Emmanuel," she said. "I love you. It's not easy for any of us, being in this time of transition with Adam. He has changed all of our lives. Look how different we are now from what we were then. We live in a different place. We have different values. We didn't know what morality was before. Now everyone is married. People want to have kids and raise them together. We building communities, a society. You can't blame yourself for what you were like before all of this happened. It was a different world then. We were different people then."

I finally looked up at Sarah. "But you've always been different, Sarah," I replied softly. "You were the reason Adam held out hope for the rest of us."

"And I wanted you, Emmanuel," Sarah said. "I always wanted you. I chose you."

I looked deeply into Sarah's eyes. They were so black yet so bright. She gazed steadily back. She had always been a pretty girl, but she seemed to grow more attractive every day. I wanted to take her back to the tent like Heber had taken Ada. But Nava was awake and she needed attention.

"We'll make a good family, the three of us," I said.

Something behind me caught Sarah's attention, and she looked up and beamed. I turned around to see Adam standing there, with Eve by his side. Standing next to Eve was Seth.

I stood up with Nava in my arms. Eve smiled, took Nava, and complimented her on how fast she was growing. Nava said "Eve," and both Adam and Eve laughed. Nava had grown very fond of the woman during the time we had been at the camp. Adam embraced me, and then Sarah, and inquired into our affairs.

"We're doing fine," I said.

Adam remarked that everyone in the camp had been busy since the night before deciding which of his sons to follow into their new communities. Then he said that most people were fascinated by Cain and Abel's communities, but that Seth's path held a charm all its own. I informed Adam that Sarah and I wanted to join Cain in the city, and Adam remarked that progress and advancement along material lines, as Cain desired, was meritorious, but that one must not forget the importance of character and integrity. This comment of Adam's stayed with me for a long time afterwards, and I thought long and hard about it. I wondered what it meant, or if Adam had meant it as a warning. Did Cain have ideas about his city that I wasn't aware of? I asked Adam if I had made the right choice in joining Cain in the city. Adam replied that as I wanted the best opportunities for my daughter, I had made a sensible decision, but that I must not forget what he had told me. Moderation, he emphasized, was important in all things, even in progress; and while material development was essential, spiritual values were the foundation of every undertaking.

These comments put me in doubt about my decision to join Cain, and I wondered what Adam meant by them. So after Adam and Eve left us to visit and speak with others, I asked Seth if he felt that I was making the right choice in going with Cain.

Cain took my daughter in his arms and looked at her. "She is a beautiful child, as I have always said. She is now proving herself to be smart and good-natured, too. You want what's best for her. For that reason, I think you do well to take her with Cain into his city."

"But you yourself are founding a different community," I said. "Don't you want to convince me to join you in your own?"
"I have already described what I am doing and what I stand for," Seth replied warmly. "I do not wish to promote myself at the expense of my brothers. Cain is my older brother and I respect him. He is a good man and he means well. He gives me no reason to tell you not to join him in the city. But if you ever want to join me and farm the land, you will be welcome. I am sure that Abel feels the same way as well."

"Thank you, Seth. You have been good to me. You've taught me much and have been instrumental in helping Sarah and I begin life together as a family. I'll never stop being grateful to you."
Seth embraced me, stood back, held me by the arms and looked into my eyes. "Our paths will cross again, Emmanuel," he said. "Life is long, and none of us knows what it has in store."

"I hope that comes to pass," I said.

When Seth left us, I looked at Sarah. "I'm worried about joining Cain in the city," I said. "I have a feeling that something's wrong."
"Did Adam, Eve or Seth tell you anything to make you think that?" Sarah asked.

"Not exactly," I said. "Seth even tells me he agrees with my decision. He says it would give the best opportunities to Nava."
"Then I wouldn't worry about it," Sarah said. "We've already decided, and informed Adam as well. Let's give Cain a chance. We can always change our minds later, right?"

"Yeah. But we'll be careful. Remember what Seth said about his community. He values character and family values above all else. And Abel values moderation and harmony with nature. If I find that, despite all of his high-minded ideas, Cain and his city stray from these important spiritual things, I will move you and Nava to a place that will better nurture your souls. I want Sarah to have opportunities, yes, but I don't want that to come at the expense of the goodness and love she takes into her heart."

15

Then Cain went out from the presence of the Lord and dwelt in the land of Nod on the east of Eden.

Genesis 4:1

Later that day, Sarah and I took Nava to a place where a group of parents were sitting with their kids. Small children were running around and playing with each other. There were also several babies crawling on the ground with their parents watching them. We placed Nava on the ground beside these other babies. She played with them and laughed with them. I watched as Nava crawled toward a little boy who was sitting on the ground and staring at the adults.

"Hi," Nava yelled at the boy. "Hi!"

Sarah laughed. "Nava's made a new friend!"

"She's quite social," I said. "She'll have a lot of friends."
The boy paid her no mind. Nava grabbed his hand and started shaking it, and then the boy looked at her and started crying. Nava let go of the boy's hand and looked at us.

"It's okay, Nava," Sarah said. The boy's mother picked him up and comforted him, and as she walked by she winked at me. I went and picked Nava up too.

"I think he's a little shy," I told my daughter. She beamed up at me.

"Let her play a little more, Emmanuel," Sarah said.

I put Nava back down with the other children. She crawled around with several less timid boys and girls. I smiled as I watched them.

"Emmanuel."

I recognized the deep voice as Cain's and looked up. He was standing next to an absolutely beautiful woman whom I had never seen before.

"Cain. Good to see you. It seems that there is a lot of interest in your city."

"And I heard from my father that you and Sara will be joining me," Cain said. "I'm so happy that is the case. You'll be of great value to our community."

"I just want Nava to have a good future," I told Cain. "And I like the idea of her growing up in an environment of ambition and progress."

"She'll have a great future," Cain assured me.

"And who is this you have with you?" Sarah asked, looking at the girl with an arm in Cain's.

"This is Leila, my wife," Cain said proudly.

"Pleased to meet you," Leila said sweetly. She was seductive and dark, with long flowing hair and an alluring figure.

"You are married?" I asked Cain, surprised.

"We will be married tonight," Cain said. "My brothers have chosen wives as well. After the ceremony, we will announce that the people will spend their last night together in the camp. The next day, we will all go our separate ways to start our communities."

"This is great news," I said. "I'm sure Leila is a very lucky girl."

"I met her two years ago," Cain said, looking down at Leila. "I told her that she would be mine one day."

"And you kept your promise," Leila said, gazing longingly at him.

"And you've been chaste all along?" Sarah asked.

"Just as my father and mother taught," Cain said. "I wouldn't break their commands."

"And I have been patient as well," Leila said. "Cain said that the best things would have to wait, but I knew he would be worth it."

"Emmanuel," Cain said. "In the city, everyone will have a different job. I want you to know that you'll be able to choose any job you wish."

"You mean everyone won't?" I asked, raising my eyebrows.

"It'll be chaos if everybody tries to pick what they are going to do," Cain said. "There will be disagreements and conflicts, and I want to avoid them. So I am going to appoint people to tasks. I am working out a system where people will rotate out of the least pleasant or desirable jobs every couple of years."

"I think that's reasonable, Emmanuel," Sarah said.

I nodded. "I guess it is. But thank you, Cain. I appreciate the freedom you are giving me. One of the reasons I wanted to come to the city was so that I would be free to do something that would give me time for my family."

"You will have plenty of that," Cain said.

Nava took a small wooden figurine from the hands of another child and the child started crying. Sarah picked Nava up and handed the toy back to the crying child, who was satiated.

"You can't do that, Nava," Sarah said calmly. "That wasn't yours." Nava started crying herself, and Sarah rocked her back and forth in her arms. "Shhh, Nava," she said. "It's okay."

"I'll see you tomorrow, Emmanuel," Cain said to me. "You, Sara and Nava can ride with Leila and I at the front of the group."

"Ride?" I asked.

"It's a surprise for my people, but my men and I have caught a herd of horses, a new animal that inhabits this land. Men can sit on their backs and ride them to travel long distances, and they can also be used as pack animals to carry supplies which can be tied to their backs."

"And how many of these horses do you have?" I asked.

"About thirty," Cain said. "Right now, they are for my best men to use. Once we start the city, we will catch more and use them to transport goods to and from the city."

"And Sarah can ride as well?" I asked.

"The three of you can ride together," Cain replied. "I've made saddles out of oxhide that will help you sit on the animals, and you can steer them with ropes of twine that are wrapped around their noses. You will direct the animal and Sarah will hold Nava and sit behind you."

"How far will we be traveling, exactly?" I asked.

"My father has told me that there is an area rich in bronze and iron about a four day's walk from here," Cain said.

"Bronze and iron?"

"Metals," Cain replied. "Hard elements found in the ground, that can be extracted and used to make tools and other goods. My father has explained to me how it works. Men must dig into the ground and remove the substances, and then they can be melted and bent into different shapes and forms."

"Interesting," I said. "Is this bronze and iron part of your plans for progress?"

"I am planning many things," Cain replied with a gleam in his eye, "Many things that my father has taught me and no one else. I will show you all of these things soon."

I looked at Sarah. "It looks like we have made the right choice," I said. "Cain is smart and capable, and he seems to have unknown wonders in store for us."

Cain smiled again. "I will see you tomorrow, then." Leila waved us goodbye as the two of them walked away.

That night, Cain, Abel and Seth were married, as promised. All three of them had beautiful brides. Adam gave a benediction afterwards, and spoke to the crowd about how happy he was with their progress since leaving Eden. They had all listened to his exhortations, taken spouses, and were now living together peacefully and faithfully. Adam hoped that the people would not forget the things he had taught them, that they would be good to each other, and remember always the values of love and morality. That night was the last night in the plain, Adam said. He was choosing several hundred men who would be his soldiers and bodyguard, whom he would train to maintain order and stability throughout the land. He announced the name of these men, who all came to the front of the crowd and accepted this new service gratefully and without exception. Then Adam said that the rest of the people would be going to their chosen communities tomorrow. Cain, Abel and Seth would break camp at dawn, and the rest of the people would follow them. Adam entrusted the people to the care of his three sons, but said that he would continue to remain at the camp, where he would set up his residence and receive whatever visitors wished to come to him in the future. Although he was now their king, he loved the people, Adam said, and he would rule them with perfect justice. No one doubted this. When Sarah and I made love that night, as we had every night, we talked about how it was our last night before beginning a new life in a new place.

"I know I'll be fine as long as you're with me," Sarah said.

"I won't fail either you or our daughter," I told her.

The next morning, we woke up before dawn and found the people breaking up into three large groups. The largest group was building around Cain. I found Cain, and as promised he was standing at the head of thirty large brown horses, each of which had a saddle on its back and was being held with a rope by a different man. Cain motioned to one of the men, who gave me the rope to his horse. It was big and muscular, but calm and gentle. It snorted when I took the rope, and then bent its head and sniffed my hair. I rubbed it on the forehead.

"Get on," Cain said. I looked at Sarah, who was holding Nava, and she nodded. So I got up onto the horse.

"Kick its sides to get it to go forward," Cain said, "And pull on the rope to make it stop. Pull the rope to the left or to the right to make it turn."

I kicked my legs and the horse started moving forward. I pulled back on the reigns and it stopped.

"Remarkable," I said.

"These are good animals, and very intelligent," Cain replied. "They will be of good use to us."

I practiced with the horse a little. I made it walk and then trot. I turned it to the right and to the left. It always stopped whenever I wanted it to. It was as if it could read my thoughts.

"Sarah and Nava can come on with you," Cain said. "These animals are very trusting and well-behaved. My father promised me that it's safe."

I jumped off the horse and took Nava from Sarah.

"I'll help you up," I said, "And then I'll give you Nava and hop on with you."

I took Sarah's hand and helped her up on the saddle. Then I handed Nava to her. The horse remained still and very calm. It took some grass in its mouth and started chewing. I hopped on in front of Sarah and held the rope.

"We'll be leaving soon," Cain said. A number of other men, many of whom I recognized, had gotten onto the other horses, each with a woman behind him. Some of the women were holding a child. There was also a large crowd behind us.

Cain stood on a rock and addressed the people. "We're leaving," he said. "It's a four day's walk to where we want to go. We will go slowly, and stop to rest every night. I look forward to starting a new life with all of you."

The people cheered. Then Cain walked up to his horse, helped Leila up onto it, and then hopped on himself. He nodded to me, and kicked his horse forward at a slow pace. I followed his lead, and so did the other men on horses and the crowd walking on foot. Overall, there were over four thousand people coming with us to found Earth's first city.

The weather was soft and temperate as we traveled. Each night, we stopped before sunset, and the men on horseback went out to hunt herds of cattle or bison and bring them back for the people. We cooked enough dinner for everyone on huge fires. We all slept out under the open sky. There were no predators or other dangers to worry us. Everyone felt happy, optimistic, and peaceful.

The land we traveled was full of different kinds of fruit trees, nuts, berries, vegetables and fields of wheat and grains through which often ran rivers or streams. Lakes and ponds also dotted the landscape, and we never had to go too far to find fresh water. The area wasn't as lush as Eden, but it was still very fertile and full of good things. I looked forward to a future in this place, and felt sure that the city would be a success.

After four days, we reached a place at the edge of a group of small hills. Cain motioned for us to stop. "Those hills over there, Emmanuel, they are where we will build the mines of bronze and iron," he told me. Then he pointed to a large plain, bounded on each side by two rivers flowing in opposite directions. "In the center of that plain, we will build our city. There are fields of wheat growing on the other side of that river," he pointed to one horizon, "and there are large herds of game on the other side of that one," he pointed to another horizon. "And beyond that, there is a forest of large trees, whose wood we will use to build our houses. My father told me that this was the perfect spot, and he was right."

"Your father's knowledge never ceases to amaze me," I said, shaking my head.

"My father has a reputation for knowledge and wisdom," Cain replied. "But he exceeds even that. He seems to know everything. There is nothing beyond his knowledge."

Cain started moving again, and led us to the plain between the rivers. Then he got off his horse, and helped Leila off as well.

"We're here, Sarah," I said. I got off the horse and helped her down. The people gathered in the plain, rejoicing to arrive at their new home. Cain gave his men instructions. "Go out and hunt for the people," he said. "They will be our guests until the city is built. Then people will begin to provide for themselves."

Cain gave a speech to mark the occasion, encouraging the people and promising them much success and prosperity in their new lives. The next day, he said, he and his men would catch more horses, and would begin transporting wood from the forest into the plain. Within a week, the people could start to build their houses. A month after that, the people would all have their homes. Then they could begin new professions that Cain himself would help them learn. For now, people could relax and enjoy themselves. Everything they needed would be provided.

Everyone cheered. Sarah, however, asked to excuse herself. I held Nava as I watched her walk away from the crowd and throw up in the grass. When she walked back, I asked her if she was alright.

"Emmanuel," Sarah said, smiling at me with radiant eyes, and holding a hand over her stomach. "I think I'm pregnant."

16

And Cain knew his wife, and she conceived and bore E'noch. And he built a city, and called the name of the city after the name of his son—E'noch.

Genesis 4:17

I brushed Sarah's hair away from her eyes, and held my hand over hers.

"How do you know?" I asked.

"I've been feeling funny lately, and my period is late."

I smiled, and looked at her tenderly. "Sarah, that's wonderful!" I said. "Nava will have a brother or sister to look after, and to look after her."

Sarah beamed at me. "Now we'll both know it's yours."

"And it won't depend upon an obscure dream of Morag's, either."

Sarah laughed. "Morag probably just turned over in his grave."

"He'd be happy to know that I'm taking care of you, and not just for a year, for a lifetime."

"Marriage is a trend you started, Emmanuel. My brothers and uncles didn't die for nothing."

"Everything has a purpose, Sarah," I replied. "Even if it's reforming someone like me."

"I've always told you that you were a good man, and I've always been right, Emmanuel."

"Even good men need guidance sometimes."

"That's why Adam is here. We all needed guidance. He helped us learn a better way to live."

"So you don't miss Eden?"

"It was comfortable there. There were no worries, no concerns. But no one cared about what they did or what the consequences were. No one was held accountable for anything. We needed a new start, and I'm glad we left. Whatever challenges this new world holds for us, we will meet them."

"It's good that Adam instilled ideas into our heads and hearts, ideas of right and wrong, of wanting to be better, of demanding more from life. If he hadn't, I don't think anyone would have wanted to leave our careless lives in Eden behind."

"It wasn't good, Emanuel, living in ignorance like that. We would kill each other, and not think anything of it. Men and women had no respect for each other, viewing each other only as objects of lust and pleasure. We have intelligence and reason, but we weren't using them in Eden."

"And so the time came for us to move on," I said. "Adam led us out of that existence, and for better or for worse, we're never going back."

"It's definitely for the better."

A man approached us and interrupted our conversation. "Emmanuel," he said. "We're catching horses to use to transport wood from the forest. A number of men have already gone with their stone hatchets to begin chopping down trees. We wanted to know if you are going to come with us."

"Of course," I said. I handed Nava to Sarah. "You two take care of each other," I said. "I'll be back before sunset."

Nava kissed me and her lips lingered on mine. "I love you, Emmanuel."

"I love you too, Sara, and I'm so lucky to be your husband."

I walked away with the man, and joined a group of about fifty men who were ready to head out into the plains. They saw me approaching, smiled and waved. I was popular among the men for being the first man to take a wife. The story of how things had played out between Sarah and I, from the very beginning, was well known. A man who had become a close friend of mine, Tahmid, came out of the group to greet me.

"Emmanuel. Cain has told us that there is a herd of horses close to the river. We won't have to travel far."

"Is Cain coming with us?" I asked.

Tahmid shook his head. "No," he replied. "Cain has to stay with the camp and oversee the affairs of the people."

"I think they'll be alright, Tahmid." It was Cain. He had joined the group.

"I'll come with you," Cain said. "I've already instructed a number of people on how to make saddles. When we return with the horses, they will be ready. We will take them to the forest immediately and begin returning the wood the men have been cutting."

"Very well," I said.

Cain slapped me on the back and smiled at me warmly. "Emmanuel," he said. "Good to see you."

"The plans for the city are progressing nicely," I replied. "Our new homes will be up in no time."

"Let us hope," Cain said.

We walked for about an hour beyond the river until we came to the herd of horses. They were just like the ones we had already caught, large and brown, with thick flowing manes.

"Easy," Cain said. "These animals are strong, but like the others, gentle and trusting. They have no reason to fear you and will not run from you. Walk up to them slowly and climb onto them. They will let us ride them back to the camp."

"We should have brought ropes," I said.

"Ropes are being prepared at the camp, along with the saddles," Cain replied. "They will be ready by the time we get back."

Along with the other men, I walked into the herd. The horses were grazing and occasionally looked up at us curiously, but otherwise paid us no mind. I walked up to one and rubbed its nose. It breathed out softly and continued to graze. I slung one arm around its pack and pulled myself on top of it.

"Put your hands around their necks and guide their movements as you would with a rope," Cain said. I held onto the horses neck and kicked my legs. It started moving forward and I turned it to the right and to the left. Then I pulled back on its neck and it stopped.
Soon the other man had gotten onto their horses too. We rode the animals back to the camp, where a large group of men and women had prepared ropes and ox-hide saddles. We fitted the animals and looked at them with pride. It was only about midday.

With the horses that we already had with us, there numbered about eighty.

"There's still time to go to the forest and bring back the first load of wood," Cain said. "Then tomorrow morning, we can begin building our houses."

Tahmid and I got onto our horses to ride with the other men to the forest. Cain didn't come with us this time. He stayed at the camp to overlook a group of men who were sharpening stones to use as knives and axes. He also wanted to go examine the site of the bronze and iron mines. So we rode off on a trot past the river and toward the forest Cain had described. As promised, within two hours we found it. About a hundred men had been working on the trees. They had already cut down a large number and chopped the wood into manageable beams. We greeted the men and each hauled several beams of wood onto our horses, tying them with ropes to the horses' sides. Then we rode back, at a slower pace, towards the camp. We got there just before sunset.

Cain met us as we arrived, and instructed us as to where to place the wood. Our work for the day done, I found Sarah. She was watching Nava play and talking with a group of women who were also caring for their young children. I was overjoyed when I saw her.

"We're making great progress, Sarah," I said. "Soon we will have our homes, and a measure of privacy."

"I don't mind it as it is now, having a community like this," Sarah replied. "We didn't have any sense of community in Eden."

"We'll still have a community when we have houses, Sarah," I said. "But we'll have our privacy as a family as well."

"You mean we'll be able to make love," Sarah said.

I laughed. "Right now we're having to go without."

Sarah smiled at me. "You know I can't wait, Emmanuel," she said.

We continued the work of transporting the wood and building the houses for the next month. Of the four thousand people in the camp, about fifteen hundred were men of working age. About two hundred of the men set about chopping wood, three hundred transporting the wood on horseback, two hundred men were responsible for hunting and cooking for the camp, four hundred men began building houses, one hundred men began preparing the bronze and iron mines, one hundred men set about creating stone tools and doing other odd jobs, and two hundred men went out to the wheat, grain, fruit and vegetable fields and started preparing farms. Cain constantly went back and forth throughout these groups of men, instructed them on their jobs, gave them practical knowledge which he had been taught by Adam, oversaw their work and generally encouraged them on their progress. The women of the camp watched the children, gathered fruits and vegetables, helped with the cooking, and helped out around the camp.

Within two months, over fifteen hundred wooden houses had been built. They all looked the same, and were built precisely according to Cain's instructions. They had two floors. On the ground floor was a room for eating, a room for cooking, and a room for storage. Small ladders led up to the second floor, which contained an area for sleeping. The houses were simple to make, and now there were enough to house each couple and family. After the houses were complete, the men set about creating other structures. They built an inn for visitors, several taverns where people could eat and drink, a building for the administration of city affairs from which Cain would govern the city, shops for butchers, carpenters and toolsmiths, and storehouses for wheat, grains, vegetables and fruits. We also dug a well and built it with stone so that people wouldn't have to walk out to the rivers all the time for water.

Sarah and I moved into a house next to Cain and Leila's. The couple insisted that we do so and said it would be their honor to be our neighbors. Sarah really enjoyed her new home. It was much better than a tent, she said, and more suited for a family. I was also relieved to have my privacy with Sarah again. Although the child in her stomach was beginning to grow, we made love for hours every night while Nava was asleep. I could not get enough of Sarah. I loved her. She gave me more than just pleasure. She gave me more than comfort. She gave me joy. She gave me love. When I was with her, when we were united as one, that was when I felt at peace. Whenever I was away from her, I felt uneasy, restless. I just wanted to be with her. I just wanted to serve her, to make her life better, to keep her safe and protected and happy. I loved my daughter for the sake of my wife. As dear to me as Nava was, as much as I was willing to sacrifice in order to raise her, Sarah was and would always be number one in my life. Sarah used to always tell me, "I was created for you." Those words had sunk deeply into my heart, so deep in fact that now I felt the same way about her. I felt that my very existence was for my wife's sake. That knowledge made me all the more devoted and faithful to her. I would never think about hurting her or disappointing her in any way. All I ever thought about was her happiness. When I brought her joy, I brought myself joy, so that was all I did.

Leila was pregnant, too. She was only about a month behind Sarah. The two women became close friends. They would spend their days together, while I was out hunting or making tools. Increasingly, I had been working on creating stone tools for farming, hunting and mining. Cain was slowly training me and enabling me to increase my skills. I had a talent for tool-making; Cain said I was the best and most skilled tool-smith in the camp. He asked me if I would like to make tool-making my profession, and I said I wouldn't mind. It was a good job; easy, relaxing, meditative, and not too demanding so that I could spend time with Sarah and my daughter. Cain promised that my job would evolve as soon as the bronze and iron mines got running. He would show me had to take the metals, melt them and forge them into even more powerful tools than the ones made of stone. I looked forward to this new opportunity. I had never seen metal before, but Cain promised me that it was marvelous. He said that it was what would make our city distinguished from all other communities, and what would make Adam proud of us.

By eleven months, Nava was saying full sentences. She was so intelligent. I was astonished by her precocity and perceptiveness. She would ask about the other parents and children in the camp, and tell us stories about interactions she had with the other children. And she was interested in my work and in the tools I made. I would take her into my shop and she would ask about the hammers, the hoes, the spears, the knives, and the other tools and I would explain to her how I made them and what they would do. She listened patiently and attentively and absorbed everything I said to her. I was astonished by her interest and knew that she would grow to be a great woman one day. I loved her more than my own heart.

Finally the time came for Sarah to give birth. When her water broke and she started having contractions, Leila came to my shop and told me what was happening. I hurried home and found Cain already there.

"She's going into labor," Cain said. "I will go find the midwives."

"I will go find them, Cain," I said.

But he held my hand and looked at me seriously. "You need to be with your wife, Emmanuel. It's no problem for me, I'll go."

When Cain arrived with two old women who assured me that they would take care of everything, Tahmid and Caleb and their wives came as well. They grinned at me.

"Exciting," Tahmid said.

"We're still waiting for our first one," Caleb said. "You're lucky."

I held Sarah's hand for hours as she gasped in pain in the presence of the midwives. Finally the time came for the child to be born, and one of the old women asked the men to leave the room.

"But I want to be with her," I said, surprised.

"The midwife is right, Emmanuel. It is more proper," Cain replied. I shook my head but left the room with the other men. I waited anxiously outside the door as I heard Sarah screaming and the midwives telling her to push and breathe. Finally, after what seemed like hours, I heard the sound of fragile cries. I rushed inside and saw the midwife handing a tiny child to Sarah.

"Emmanuel, it's a boy," Sarah said, smiling and with tears in her eyes. Whether her tears were of joy or pain I did not know.

I breathed a sigh of relief. "Are they both okay?" I asked the midwife.

"They'll both be fine," the woman said. "As for you, you will now have another man to share the house with."

I smiled and embraced the old woman, who was a little shocked. Cain, Tahmid and Caleb came into the room. They congratulated me and Sarah.

"You're family is growing, Emmanuel," Cain said. "I only hope that Leila and I will be so lucky."

"You will be," I replied.

"Emmanuel, do you want to hold him?" Sarah asked.

"I would love to, Sarah," I said.

I took the child, wrapped in beaver skin, into my arms.

"What will you name him?" Caleb asked.

I looked at Sarah. "Choose the name, Emmanuel," she said softly. "Name your son whatever you like."

I looked at the boy. I loved him to death. I wanted to teach him everything. I wanted to help him grow into a man. A strong man. "I name him Nadir," I said. "It means, 'oath.' I make my oath right now to him, in front of all of you, that I will guide him, protect him, love him, and be the best father any man could be."

Sarah nodded and smiled. Everyone else cheered.

"Emmanuel, if I may," Cain said.

I handed Nadir to Adam's son. He held him tenderly in his hands. "Son of Emmanuel," he said, "May you grow to be tall and strong. May you grow to become the finest of men, the pride of your father, and the joy of your city."

Then Cain handed the child back to his mother, embraced me, and led the others out of the room.

"Let them have their privacy, now," he said.

Alone with my wife and two children now, I gazed at them for a moment, and laughed for joy.

17

And as for Zillah, she also bore Tubal-Cain, an instructor of every craftsman in bronze and iron.

Genesis 4:22

I enjoyed life greatly with my wife, my daughter and my infant son. Nava adored her little brother and gave him lots of attention. "Daddy!" she would say to me. "Nadir smiled at me!"

"Of course he smiled at you, Nava!" I would say. "Who wouldn't?"

She would smile and hug my leg, and I would pick her up and twirl her in the air.

Sarah, too, found great joy and pleasure in our growing family. Her whole world was Nava, Nadir and I. She didn't need or want anything or anybody else to keep her happy. The amount of love and trust she showed me was incredible. She was assured of my love, and she knew that I would never let her down. As a family, the four of us depended on each other, loved each other, and rejoiced each other's hearts.

About a month after Nadir was born, Cain informed me that the bronze and iron mines were ready. He told me that he wanted me to be the city's first metalworker and metal tool smith. I replied that I would gladly do this job. So Cain ordered some men to bring chunks of iron and bronze from the mines to my shop. He also brought in a large stone cauldron that he had ordered made for my work. Then patiently, over the course of several days, he showed me how to melt the metals in the cauldron over a fire, how to pour the molten metals into casts chipped from stone and covered in wax, and how to cool the metal and hammer it into shape as it cooled so that it would take the form I desired. In this way, I was able to make many tools for farming, construction work, digging, cutting, chopping and hunting that were even better than the stone ones I had made before.

Cain introduced another use for the metals, too. He brought me stone casts that were imprinted with a small, circular shape. By pouring molten bronze into the disc-like imprints in the cast, I was able to produce small discs that Cain called coins. Up until that time, people in the city freely gave each other anything anyone might need. If someone needed food, the farmers would send it to them. If someone needed tools, I would provide them. There were no questions asked, and no greed. People took it as a matter of course to cooperate. But Cain thought that this system wouldn't work properly in the long term, so he introduced a system he called money. Each of the goods people produced, Cain said, would be given a value in terms of coins. For example, an iron hammer I made could be given a value of three bronze coins. If someone wanted to receive a hammer from me, he would have to give me three coins. Then I, in turn, could use those coins to purchase other things I needed, such as food or clothes made by the cloth workers. Using money, Cain promised, the city would become much more stable and efficient. So I set about making as many bronze coins as I could so that Cain could distribute an even initial amount throughout the city.

In the mornings, I would wake up with Sarah and the children at dawn. I would play with Nava and Nadir, and take care of one of them while Sarah breastfed the other. We would talk and laugh and play. Then we would have breakfast, which was usually bread or oats with milk from the cows which the herders had caught and domesticated, fruits, berries and sometimes meat. After about an hour or two, I would go to the shop, where I would work until lunchtime. Then I would go to the butcher, get some meat, and come home to roast it over the fire. Sarah would cook vegetables as well, and we would eat together. Occasionally Nava would eat with us, as she was about old enough to be weaned. After lunch I would take Sarah and the children out for a walk through the fields and meadows outside of the city, or for a stroll by the river. Occasional Cain and Leila, or Tahmid and Caleb and their wives, or other friends in the city, would come with us. Afterwards, I would go back to the shop for the afternoon, and stay there until just before sunset. It was a relaxing and peaceful job, and I found it very easy and restful. I would make tools and appliances of bronze and iron, or whatever things people requested, and often people would come into the shop and exchange the items they wanted or had requested for bronze coins. As I had been the one to make the coins, I had plenty already, but no one in the city was ever at a lack for money or anything they needed to live on or enjoy.

About two months after Nadir was born, Cain and Leila's child was born. It was a boy, and Cain named him Enoch. Enoch was a fine boy, big and robust and bright, with thick, black hair and a calm smile. Everybody in the city came to congratulate Cain and Leila on their newborn child, and Cain loved Enoch so much that he named the city Enoch after him. So from that day forward, we lived in the city of Enoch.

After Enoch was born, often in the evenings Sarah and I would take Nava and Nadir to Cain and Leila's home, and we would reflect on the budding lives of our new families. Cain had experience with families because his mother and father, Adam and Eve, who were Eden's first committed couple, had been together his whole life, and he had grown up in a loving home. Sarah and I had both grown up on our own, essentially orphans like most of the rest of Eden, although Sarah had her uncles and brothers to look after her, which made her something like a princess. So Cain would tell us stories about how his parents raised him and his brothers, and we would consult on the challenges of family life together.

For the most part, Sarah and I didn't have any conflicts as a married couple. We were both so dedicated and committed to our relationship and our family that we went out of our way to support each other and make each other happy. Neither of us really had any complaints. But we had noticed that not all of the families of Enoch were living in such a way. There seemed to be many couples that were growing tired of each other, or were becoming unhappy. Sometimes men weren't there emotionally for their wives, or they didn't give adequate love and attention to their children. This problem was exacerbated by the fact that people were distracted by the system of money that Cain had introduced. Before money existed, people had always had all they needed already provided for them. When people worked, it was only on projects that they had an immediate interest in. For example, people would hunt or build a hut. The work they did had a practical purpose. But with money and the new system of work that Cain had introduced into the city, the concept of work became a little more abstract. Cain had chosen a job or task for every man in the city. He had tried to match everyone to their strengths, but occasionally people were unhappy with the jobs they were assigned. Cain alleviated this discontent by promising that every job would only be held for three years. After that, people could rotate out to a different job if they didn't like the ones that they already had. He had also promised that the most difficult jobs would receive the most money. For example, if someone was a farmer or a miner, they would receive more money than people with less laborious work.

With their new jobs, however, men started to get anxious about how much money they got. For the first time, they actually had to worry about having the means for livelihood and enjoyment. Before, prosperity wasn't something that certain people had and others lacked. Now, people began thinking about the fact that eventually, some people would have more money than others. Men began to compete with each other in their work. Some men worked harder and longer, becoming absorbed in their work so that they could amass more money. This took a toll on their family lives. They began to lose track of reality, of their sense of what was really important. They began to value their wives and children less than the money they made at work. They also began to view other people differently. Since everyone now had a different task, people were no longer just men anymore. Now there were farmers, miners, butchers, cloth makers, metalworkers. Some people were respected more than others based solely on the jobs they held. There was division among the people again. Before, in Eden, people would kill each other based on the smallest misunderstanding, but they still viewed others as their equals. Now, killing had been outlawed, and people refrained from it, but a new problem had appeared: prejudice. People viewed each other through mental lenses that represented some as lower and some as higher, some as insiders and others as outsiders. Men started to become bigoted and arrogant. Some took inordinate pride in their status and wealth, and others became jealous and discontent. All of these things poisoned not only the social life of the city, but also family life and relations between men and their wives and children. To remedy, or at least alleviate, this problem, Cain introduced something new into the life of the city, something that we had never had in Eden. He showed the people how to press grapes to make grape juice that could be stored in wooden cups and containers, and then how to store the grape juice and let it ferment so that it turned into wine. Wine, he said, would calm people's minds and get all of the new and confounding thoughts about money and class out of their heads.

There were orchards of wild grapes growing about an hour's distance from the city, and Cain had over a hundred farmers devote themselves to growing grape for wine. He also set up two buildings as breweries and started introducing wine to the taverns. After work, people would go to the taverns, drink wine and have a good time with each other. This eased the growing tensions among the people of the city and introduced a new sense of camaraderie. I went with Sarah to the tavern on several occasions, and we tried the wine. The intoxicating sensation that resulted from drinking several cups was pleasing in a sense, but I didn't like the fact that it made people do ridiculous things. It took away one's intelligence. Maybe, I thought, it was good for the other men who were already having problems with anxiety and stress, but I was happy with my family and work. And while I didn't mind going to the tavern every once in a while with Sarah, it wasn't really a place for the kids, and I wanted to spend my time with them. I wondered about the men who spent all of their time after work at the tavern. What would become of their families? It clearly wasn't going to help their relationships with their wives and children. I wanted to bring this concern to Cain, but after thinking about it I decided to keep my concerns to myself. It wasn't my responsibility to define how other men spent their time or treated their families. I was responsible for one life and one life only, and that was my own. How I conducted myself, and how I cared for my family, was my own business, and my only concern.

However, I still worried about the way the city was turning out. I discussed the problem with Sarah over dinner one night.

"I wanted to come and build this city with Cain because he promised progress," I said. "I wanted a better life for my children. And there has been progress—we have organized lives, a home, new technologies and materials with which to live—but it's not necessarily of the kind that I think will benefit Nava and Nadir. This system of money and trade that Cain has introduced, I can see that it's necessary, but is it really making the people of Enoch into better people? I think it's made us worse. People are becoming selfish and self-centered. They are less friendly and they are competing with each other. And now to remedy all of this, Cain has introduced wine. Look how it's making people act. It doesn't take a genius to see that families are going to start falling apart. This isn't the progress that Cain promised. People aren't advancing in morals. Integrity and character is falling apart. We barely led better lives for a year."

Sarah tried to reassure me. "I don't know about the rest of the city, Emmanuel, but I know that you haven't changed. You're still the same person you were after you met Adam for the first time. You're still the husband and father I've always known you'd be. Whatever happens, I know you'll do the right thing. And I don't doubt your choice for bringing us here. If you ever want to leave, I'll go with you."

I felt grateful to Sarah for being so affirming and supportive. "I don't want to leave the city yet. Things haven't gotten to that point. I'm just worried about where everyone is heading, that's all. If people start acting up or getting worse, I'll talk about it with Cain. Then if that still doesn't help, I won't hesitate to move you and our children to live with Abel or Seth. I know that Cain is Adam's son, but he isn't Adam. He's a great man, but I'm not so sure about the direction he's leading his city in. We're making progress, but progress of the wrong kind. Our spirits aren't coming along for the ride."

"I know that Nava, Nadir and I will be fine with you leading us, Emmanuel," Sarah said. "Don't hesitate to do what you feel you have to do. You said that Cain is great, but you are great too. Make strong decisions based on what you know is right, and we will follow you."

I gave Sarah a kiss and held her tight, and vowed to do what was best for her.

18

His brother's name was Jubal. He was the father of all those who play the harp and flute.

Genesis 4:21

I was making iron tools one day at work when Miyka, a farmer, came into the shop.

"Good afternoon, Miyka!" I said. "What brings you here today?"

"I need a hoe for work, Emmanuel. One of those new iron ones you've been making."

I smiled, and told him to come around back. "I just so happened to make several iron hoes today. I can sell you one for three bronze coins."

"That will be a simple matter, Emmanuel."

I brought Miyka to the back of the shop and showed him the hoes. "These are strong, durable and very efficient. You will be able to dig up much dirt with this, and easily. It will not break, and you will not strain your muscles."

"The muscles are always strained when one is farming, Emmanuel."

"I know, Miyka. How has work been recently?"

I picked up an iron hoe with a wooden handle and Miyka examined it. "It has been difficult. I work with much labor and sweat of the brow. The ground always needs working. The sun is hot and the air is humid some days."

I looked at Miyka's rippling arm muscles. "You are a strong young man. You can handle it, I'm sure. Tell me, how are the harvests?"
"The harvests are plentiful. My fields are yielding much wheat, oats, and corn. I am also able to sell them for many bronze coins. I am prospering greatly."

"I am glad to hear that. What do you say about the hoe?"
Miyka handed the tool back to me. "I think it's finely made. I'll buy two of them, if that is okay with you."

I smiled. "That is fine, my friend. I have plenty. Say, do you have horses or oxen?"

"I have a few," Miyka said. "Why?"

"I have created something new, based on instructions that Cain gave me. Here, let me show you."

I led Miyka to another room at the back of the shop, where several large projects were being stored. I showed him a large piece of jagged iron that was supported by wooden beams attached to several ropes.

"What is it?" Miyka asked.

"It's called a plow," I said. "You attach it to your horse or oxen, and let the animal drag it across the fields. It digs and breaks the earth for you, so you can plant your seeds without having to do all the labor manually."

MIyka looked at the plow with wonder. "That will make my work a lot easier," he said. "How much is it?"

"Ten bronze coins," I said. "But since I like you, I'll give it to you for seven."

"It's a deal," Miyka said, shaking my hand. He couldn't believe how much this new tool would help him. I took him to the front and let him pay.

"Thirteen bronze coins," I said.

Miyka took out a pouch from his pocket and pain me the sum. "Farming is hard work," he said. "I can't wait until Cain rotates me to another job."

"That will be great," I assured him. "Until then, I hope these new tools help."

Miyka smiled and shook his head. "They will," he agreed.

I helped Miyka carry the plow to his home, which was about a five minute's walk away. Once we were there, Miyka told me to come to the tavern that night.

"Do you much like going to the tavern?" Miyka asked me, doubtfully.

"No, I don't fancy it at all," I said. "I much prefer spending time with my family every chance I get. My family needs my time, love and attention. What do the people from the tavern need from me? Let the men who are incompetent in their family affairs go there and get drunk. It's better for no one else."

"I thought so," Miyka said thoughtfully. "Men say you stay away from the taverns, and I haven't seen you there myself. At any rate, there is something new happening there tonight."

I raised my eyebrows. "Oh?" I asked. "And what is that?"

"There is a man named Jubal," Miyka said. "Have you heard of him?"

"Ah, yes, I know Jubal," I said. "He is a craftsman, is he not? Cain has him set up in a shop, making things out of wood. I hear all sorts of new, innovating and interesting things have been coming out of his shop."

Miyka nodded. "Yes, that is the one," he affirmed. "Well, this Jubal has created something never seen before, something that he said will add to the enjoyment and atmosphere of the taverns, as well as to the general life of the city."

"If it is anything like wine, I'd think we were rather better off without it," I said. "But anyway, what has he made?"

"He calls them musical instruments," Miyka said. "He has created two different kinds. They are instruments that make pleasing sounds and noises, that can be played along with songs. They are greatly entertaining and can be used to lead the people in dance as well."
I studied Miyka. "Musical instruments," I said thoughtfully. "Maybe Sarah would be pleased to see them as well."

Miyka laughed. "They are to be heard, not seen, Emmanuel. Anyway, come today to the tavern and see what you think. Miyka will be unveiling them. If you like what you hear, bring Sarah and the two of you can enjoy the music together."

I thanked Miyka warmly. "I will do that, my friend. For now, I should be going back to the shop. Good luck with your new tools."
"Thank you, Emmanuel," he replied. "You're a good man, you know."

I laughed as I walked back toward my shop, and waved Miyka goodbye. "That's what my wife, Sarah, has always said. I can only hope that she is right."

After work that evening, I went to the tavern. A crowd was gathered there, drinking and socializing and having a good time unwinding from the day's stress. Most of the people there were men, but a few had brought their wives and were drinking with them. When I walked in, I noticed Cain among the tavern's inhabitants.

Cain immediately saw me and came over to greet me.

"Emmanuel!" he said. "How good of you to come. Miyka stopped by and told me that you sold him one of your plows. Your tools are going to greatly help the inhabitants of this city."

"I am sure they will, Cain. I am only happy to be able to carry on my profession and provide for my family. I hear there are going to be musical instruments at the tavern today."

Cain smiled back at me, a sheen of sweat on his forehead. He had evidently been drinking. "Yes, inventions of Jubal. It will be a good surprise for the people." He looked around him. "Jubal? Where are you?"

A man came over with two drinks in his hand. He had been consorting with several other men. "Cain!" he said, handing a cup to the leader of the city. "This is for you." Then Jubal noticed me watching him. "Emmanuel!" he said. "Come here to hear my musical instruments?"

"I just wanted to see what all the commotion is about, Jubal," I replied. "But I'm sure they're fine."

Jubal grinned at me. "You'll like them, Emmanuel, I promise. Great for setting the mood for a fine, romantic night."

I nodded. "If it is as you say, I'll be sure to bring my wife."

"Bring your wife, or another's. It makes no difference. With my instruments, there will be plenty of love to go around." Jubal laughed at his own wit. I shook my head.

"You have a wife too, Jubal," I said. "She wouldn't like to hear you talk like that."

Cain agreed. "We have laws in this city, Jubal. Men are to know their own wives only. I don't even want to hear you joking about living otherwise."

Jubal sobered. "Yes, Cain. Whatever you say. Now, let me introduce my new instruments to the loving people of this tavern."

Cain took a sip of his wine as Jubal walked to the back of the tavern and out of sight. "He means well," he said. "His instruments will help with the spirit of this city."

"As the wine has?" I asked. "I don't like the direction the men are heading in these taverns, Cain. This is no place for families."

"Men have been faithful to their wives," Cain replied. "I've had no cases of adultery. People just need to wind down sometimes."

"It's best to wind down with your wife and kids," I said gravely. "Or else a man and his family will only grow distant and apart."

Cain tried to reassure me. "I'll make sure that things don't get out of control," he replied. "I'm watching over my city. Everyone will be fine."

"People of Enoch's finest tavern!" Jubal's voice could be heard clearly as he stood on a raised platform at one end of the room. "These are my friends, Moss and Omer."

Two men holding strange wooden instruments in their hands bowed before the crowd. Jubal continued.

"They are holding the new instruments I have made for your entertainment. In Moss's hands is a flute."

Moss was holding a long, tube-like instrument with holes along the sides. He placed it in his mouth and blew into it, moving his fingers as he blew. A high-pitched sound came out, which rose and fell as the man plugged the various holes with his fingers. The people cheered when they heard this.

"And in Omer's hands, is a harp."

Omer was holding a large wooden frame with strings of various lengths attached. He plucked the strings one by one, and the vibrations made sounds of varying frequencies. He brushed his fingers along the strings, and a heavenly sound came out of the harp. Everyone cheered again.

Cain clapped. "Isn't that great?" he asked. "Jubal is a genius. I never would have thought of it."

"It's pretty impressive," I said. "Now I'd like to see if Moss and Omer can make music come out of these instruments."
Jubal spoke again. "Now," he said. "That's not all. I have been training Moss and Omer in the playing of these instruments. They will now play a song for you."

Everyone cheered. When they quieted down, Moss started playing his flute, fast and loud. An intricate tune emerged, and people clapped along. Then Omer joined in with his harp. He played with all ten fingers, plucking the strings in a distinct rhythm that blended in with that of Moss's flute. The two men played to a tune well known among the men of the tavern.

Cain laughed, and clapped his hands to the rhythm. "Sing along!" he called out the listeners.

The men and women listening to the musicians began singing the words to the song they were playing. Their voices rang out in unison with the music emerging from the harp and the flute. "Beautiful!" Jubal said over the sound of the people's voices. "I am glad you like it so much! Free drinks for everyone!"

People cheered and continued singing as the bartenders handed out more drinks to everyone in the tavern. A barmaid offered me a mug and I declined. "No, thank you," I said. Everyone else drank and continued singing. After the song was over, Moss and Omer played another song, and another. Afterward, Cain spoke to the people. "We will need a number of musicians to play at our taverns," he said. "If any man thinks he might have a talent with the harp and the flute, let him come to me tomorrow, and I will have Jubal set him up with an instrument. You will be paid handsomely for your performances." Everyone cheered, and Jubal bade the men continue playing. As the people of the tavern had more drinks and listened to the music, I quietly escaped the tavern and made my way home, where Sarah and the kids were waiting.

"You're an hour later than usual," Sarah said, when I walked in.

"Where have you been?"

"I've been at the tavern, Sarah," I said. "Jubal has made musical instruments, that a number of men played for the first time today. Cain was there to introduce the new music to the people. He is asking for people to train as musicians so that music can be played in all of the taverns. I wanted to see what is was like so that I could bring you if it was any good."

Sarah looked at me curiously. "And was it, Emmanuel?" she asked. I nodded. "It sounded good. But it just goes along with the wine enjoyed by men who have too much stress in life. You know that I would rather spend my time with you, Nava and Nadir."

Sarah smiled. "I know you would, Emmanuel. Do you think the music is something that I would like to hear?"

"I don't know," I said. "I don't think so. It's not that great. But I'll take you tomorrow, and you could see what you think."

"I would like that," Sarah said.

"Can I come too, daddy?" Nava looked at me beseechingly.

I picked my daughter up and held her in my arms. "The tavern is no place for you, Nava," I responded warmly. "It's no place for families. In my opinion, it's no good place at all. I'm just going to take your mother tomorrow to show her what the people are up to. Afterward, we'll come home and spend our time with you and your brother."

Nava buried her face in my chest. "Okay, daddy," she said. "I missed you today."

"I missed you too, sweetheart. What did you do?"

"I helped take care of Nadir," she said. "And I played with mommy."

"You did!" I said. "That is very good of you! And did Nadir enjoy your company?"
Nava nodded. "The child adores his older sister," Sarah said. "Doesn't he, Nava?"

"He's my best friend," Nava affirmed.

I laughed. "That is so wonderful, Nava. Nadir will always be your best friend. He will always be here to protect you, even if I'm not around anymore."

"But I want you to always be around," Nava said.

"I'll be around as long as I can, my daughter," I replied. "But I just want you to know that no matter what, there will always be someone to take care of you."

Nava smiled sweetly. "I know," she said.

I put Nava down and picked up Nadir. The beautiful baby boy smiled broadly at me and giggled as I tickled his chin. "I'm so proud of you, my son," I said to him. "Thank you for taking care of your mother and sister while I was gone today."

"He was very hungry," Sarah said. "He ate and ate. Do you see how fast he is growing?"

I nodded. "He will be a big and strong man. And look at how good-natured he is. He will be a good and fine man, too."

Sarah smiled and took the child from my arms. She rocked him and spoke to him lovingly. "You will be a fine man one day, won't you? And look, you're being raised by the best."

19

So the Lord said to Cain, "Why are you angry? And why has your countenance fallen? If you do well, will you not be accepted? And if you do not do well sin lies at the door. And its desire is for you, but you should rule over it."

Genesis 4:6-7

The next day at the shop, I had four more men come in looking for plows. I sold the two that I had in stock, and took an order for the other men at ten bronze coins a piece. For the rest of the day, I worked on building plows. I made two, and the men who had ordered them returned and took them off my hands. They promised that they would tell their friends, and that I would have many more orders soon.

After work I went straight home to take Sarah to the tavern. I wanted to show her the instruments. Nava wanted to come too, but we left her and Nadir with Leila. We thanked Leila for watching them and told her we'd be back soon.

At the tavern, people were drinking and laughing and crowding around the tables. In the back, Moss and Omer were playing the flute and harp. They were playing a different tune today, a faster and freer one, and men were becoming giddy with the sound. Many had brought their wives who were curious to hear the music. A waitress offered us drinks and I bought one for myself and one for Sarah. We sat down and listened to the melody the musicians were playing.

"So?" I asked Sarah. "What do you think?"

She took a sip of her drink, then looked at me. "It has potential," she said. "But the melody they are playing doesn't do much for me."
I frowned. "Me neither. It's a promiscuous tune. Could be much better if only they had the right spirit."

I took a sip of my drink and continued listening. "It's terrible, actually," I said. "It's giving me a headache."

Sarah laughed. "Thanks for bringing me anyway."

A friend of mine, Yered, spotted us and sat down at our table. There was a woman with him, who also sat down.

They were both drunk and laughing.

"Yered," I said. "This is not your wife. Where is Eila?"
Yered laughed again. "She's at home, with our son," he said dismissively.

The woman smiled at me. "Yered's wife didn't want to join in all of the fun. I'm Hava."

I frowned again. Sarah spoke up.

"Not much fun we're having here. Things are getting a little crazy."

"Oh, come on," Yered said, holding Hava by the hand and standing up. "Dance with us."

I looked at him dubiously. "With you?"

"With Hava and I," Yered said.

I gave Sarah a look. She shook her head.

"Forget them," Hava said, drawing closer to Yered. "Show me a fun time."

The song changed to a new one, and Hava and Yered started dancing ridiculously together on the wooden floor. A number of other couples saw them and joined in, dancing together as well.

"I know there's no law against dancing with another woman," I said to Sara. "But what would Yered's wife think?"

"Poor woman," Sarah said, looking at the table. "And she's at home watching their child."

"There's not much of interest here," I said to Sarah. "Do you want to go home?"

"Yeah," Sarah said. "Let's just finish our drinks."

We continued to sit, sipping our drinks, when the song changed again and more couples joined in the dancing. Several waiters cleared tables from the back of the room, where the musicians were playing, and set up a little dance floor where men and women let loose with each other. I snorted.

"Elegant," I said. Sarah laughed.

Then a man came up to our table, and greeted us. He was drunk. "My name's Eleazar," he said. "Why don't you two come up and dance with me?"

"I think you've had one too many drinks, my friend," I said softly. "Maybe you'd better go home."

"Oh come on," Eleazar said. "And who are you, pretty lady?" He was talking to Sarah. "Why don't you come and dance with me."

"No thank you," Sarah said calmly.

"Look Eleazar, go and find someone else to dance with. You're talking to my wife."

"Just one dance with a pretty lady," Eleazar insisted. I was losing my patience. I got up and stood between him and Sarah. Then I pushed him back with both arms.

"You have a wife," I said firmly. "Go and find her. You shouldn't be dancing with anyone else."

"Why can't I just have yours for a dance?" Eleazar said with a grin. "Just one dance."

He was really drunk, but I had had enough. I curled my hand into a fist, drew it out to my side and slugged him with a right uppercut to the jaw. He wasn't expecting that at all. He fell backward, stunned, and crashed into a table, knocking over several drinks. Several men and women got up from the table and laughed at the fallen man, who had hit the back of his head pretty hard. Eleazar picked himself up and staggered around. Then he started laughing. A woman came up to him, held his hand, and the two started dancing.

I sat back down at the table. "Are you done with your drink yet?" I asked Sarah.

"Almost."

A few minutes later, Sarah was finished and we got up and left the tavern.

"That was crazy," Sarah said.

"Let's go pick up Nava and Nadir," I said.

We stopped by Cain and Leila's house and found our kids playing with Enoch.

"Nava's such a helpful little girl," Leila said, radiantly. "She's helped me watch the two little ones since you two left."

"She's a good girl," I agreed. "I'm so proud of my daughter."

"She's being raised by the best," Sarah said.

I leaned toward Leila. "She always says that," I whispered.

Leila laughed. "So you went to the tavern? Did you see Cain?"

I looked at Sarah. "No," I said. "Cain wasn't there."

"I didn't see him either," Sarah said. "I think I would have noticed him."

"He must be still at work, then," Leila said. "Cain's been really busy lately."

"It's late," I said. "What time does he usually come home?"

"Around this time," Leila said. "If you two stay a little while, you might catch him."

"No, that's all right, I think we're going to go home," Sarah said. "Thanks for watching the kids."

"Happy to help the two of you out," Leila said. She smiled warmly as we left her house and walked next door to our own.

I didn't go to the tavern again that week. I received over thirty orders for plows, so I spent the next week making them. I had gotten proficient and skilled and was making four or five each day. About a week later, I decided to head over to the tavern after work to see how things were progressing there.

The layout of the tavern had been adjusted, so that there was a space in the back in front of the musicians for people to dance together. There was also a raised platform beside the musicians where scantily clad women were dancing. Men were drinking and laughing and watching the women. Wives weren't there with their husbands as they had been last time.

I found Jubal, who was talking with several men as the musicians played and the half-naked women danced.

"Emmanuel!" he said. "Good of you to come here. I haven't seen you in some time. Heard some man got in a row with you over your wife."

"That's not why I haven't been back," I said. "I haven't been back because this tavern has become a pigpen. And what is the meaning of these women? The men who come here have wives. These women have husbands, for God's sake."

Jubal tried to calm me down. "Men and women aren't allowed to have sex unless they're married," he said. "There's no law against dancing or watching each other dance."

"It goes against the spirit of Adam's teachings," I said. "And it's low. These men and women should be thinking of their families."

"We're all a family in this city, Emmanuel," Jubal persisted. "Don't be so sour. I'm just helping people have a good time."

"This isn't a good time," I told Jubal. "This is immorality."

Jubal averted his gaze. "Hey look Emmanuel, I'll see you around. Enjoy the music."

He walked over to the other side of the tavern, and started talking with several drunken men. I looked over at the dancers. There were eight of them, all of them beautiful, their bellies, shoulders and thighs showing. All of them had husbands.

One of the women eyed me seductively, looked down at her breasts, and moved her abdomen rhythmically. I asked a waiter for a drink, and sat down at an empty table. I needed to think things over.

This wasn't the place I wanted my daughter and son to grow up in. I would have to bring this up with Cain. He would do something about it. I looked around. He wasn't here. I wondered where he was.

The waiter brought me a drink. I took a sip as I watched the men who were watching the dancers. I wondered where these people's kids were.

Caleb sat down across from me.

"Emmanuel," he said. "Fancy seeing you here."

"It wasn't too long ago that we gathered together and fought Morag and his men," I told my old friend. "Back then, we were different. We didn't have morals. We didn't have families. We valued nothing but ourselves and our own pleasure. But we changed. We grew. Adam taught us right from wrong. Or at least I thought he did. And now I see that we're going back to where we were before. The old Emmanuel, he would have enjoyed this. He would have loved those women up there, and would have made love to them when the night was over. But I am not the old Emmanuel any more. Who I am now, this Emmanuel can't stand the sight of this. It's wrong, Caleb."

Caleb looked at me seriously. "I agree, Emmanuel. I don't like this either. But these men, they have nothing against it. And Cain has nothing against it."

"Where is Cain?" I asked. "Does he ever come here?"

"He was here yesterday," Caleb replied. "I think it was his idea to bring these dancers. He said they were beautiful women and that men shouldn't be deprived of their gifts."

I was incredulous. "Cain said that?" I asked. "The son of Adam?"

"You think too highly of him, Emmanuel," Caleb replied coolly. "He's never been the best or most moral man. Everyone was all taken in by his lofty concepts of progress and the city. But look around you. This is what it's amounted too. We should have stuck with Abel or Seth."

I agreed, but I was too stunned to reply.

"I'm going to get another drink," Caleb said. "Do you want one?"

"No thanks."

Caleb got up, and I sat there with my hands in my head. What was this city to which I had brought my wife and children?

"You okay?" the sound of a woman's voice broke through my meditations. I looked up to see one of the scantily clad dancers sitting at the table across from me. She had dark brown hair and auburn eyes. She was wearing lipstick and eye shadow that made her alluring figure even more seductive. The strap of her gown had fallen over one of her shoulders, exposing one of her nipples.

I stared at her. "Your breast," I said carelessly.

"What?" the woman asked.

"Your breast is showing." My voice was deadpan.

"Oh," the woman chuckled. "Sorry." She pressed her breast up with the palm of her hand, then pulled her gown over it. "Is that better?"

"Why are you here?" I asked. I didn't want to play any games.

"You just looked lonely, that's all," the woman said. She reached out her hand and placed it over mine, which was resting on the table.

I pulled back my hand. "You were busy dancing just a minute ago. I won't ask you again. Why are you here?"

The woman sighed, and looked down. "Jubal told me to come see you," she confessed. "He said you needed to have some fun."

"Jubal?" I asked. I looked across the room to where Jubal was standing. I caught his eye, and then he turned and started talking to someone else.

"Look," she said, "my husband won't be expecting me until late tonight. If you want to leave with me…"

"No, thank you," I said. "Go and tell Jubal that this is real low, even for him."

The woman seemed hurt. "You don't think I'm beautiful?" she asked.

"This is what happens when you put yourself out there for people who don't care about you," I said to her. "Your self-esteem gets all wrapped up in what they say and do, and then you get hurt when they don't love you the way you need love. That's why we started having families in the first place. So we'd have a safe place to find love."

"My husband doesn't love me," the woman said sadly.

"Then you should find another husband." I got up. I knew the woman couldn't do that, but I had had enough.

"You're leaving?" the woman asked.

"Look, if you'll take my advice, stop dancing here. Forget about the tavern and the drunken men who come here. Go home and be with your family."

I looked over at Jubal again. He was looking at me and frowning. I turned around and walked out of the tavern.

I went over to Cain and Leila's house. Leila was playing with Enoch, and Sarah was there with Nava and Nadir. "Is Cain here?" I asked. "Emmanuel," Sarah said. She came up to me and gave me a hug.

I hugged her back. "Hi, sweetheart."

"Cain hasn't come home," Leila said. "Sarah was just here keeping me company."

"Do you know where he is?" I asked.

"He hasn't been around much, lately," Leila said. "I guess he's probably at work."

"I'm unhappy with how things are going at the tavern," I said. "If this is the social life of the city, I don't want to be a part of it. I need to go talk this over with Cain right now."

Leila looked stricken. "Cain's been different lately, Emmanuel," she said. "Maybe you can talk things over with him."

"That I will," I said.

Sarah smiled at me. "Come back soon," she said.

I grinned at her, picked Nava up, and told her how much I loved her. Then I gave Nadir a pat on the head and told him I'd be right back. I headed to where Cain's office was. The city's headquarters. Light was coming out of the windows. Cain was inside. I was so preoccupied with what I was going to say to him that I didn't think of knocking. I just walked in the door. He wasn't in his office. I walked past it into one of the back rooms.

The room was lit with two oil lamps. Rare ones that Cain had had made especially made for himself. Cain was standing with two other men at one end of the room. He looked up at me, looked surprised for a moment, and then smiled. "Emmanuel," he said.

But my attention was caught by what was happening on the other side of the room. There were three women there. Three beautiful, naked women. They were posing provocatively and stroking and kissing each other.

The women looked up at me and stopped what they were doing. Cain waved them on. "Continue," he said.

Then he looked at me. "Come here, Emmanuel," Cain said. "it's almost over, but by all means, enjoy the show."

"Stop," I said to the women, commandingly. I could feel my face turning red as I struggled to control my anger. The naked women stopped and looked up at Cain, questioningly.

Cain relented. "Get dressed and go home," he said. He turned to the men beside him. "You two as well. I have to talk to my friend."

The men nodded and left the room, the women behind them. "Your friend?" I asked. "Is that how you're going to make this all go away? I followed you here, Cain. I helped you build this city. I thought you would give me better than this."

"We're not allowed to have sex with other women, Emmanuel," Cain replied calmly. "There's nothing wrong with watching them have sex with each other."

I fixed him with a stare. "That's what Jubal told me, too," I said. "Did he learn that from you?"

"I haven't broken any rules, Emmanuel," Cain said. "I still have my integrity."

"Integrity?" I said, astounded. "Don't tell me about integrity, Cain. You promised progress in this city, but things have gone too far. This isn't progress, this is corruption."

"Look, I'm sorry to disappoint you, Emmanuel," Cain said. "You're a good man, you really are. But if you just bear with me a little while, you'll see that things aren't as bad as they seem to you right now. Everything is really going to be alright. I think you're blowing things out of proportion a little bit."

"Put a restraint on the drinking in the taverns, Cain," I said firmly. I had no delusion that he would actually listen to me, but I had to tell him anyway. "Put an end to the dancing. Tell men to honor their wives and their families. And for God's sake, make sure women have their clothes on when they're in front of you."

Cain's expression and tone changed. He suddenly turned cold and distant. "You're not my leader, Emmanuel," he said. "I'm yours. Don't tell me what to do."

"If you were a leader, you'd lead," I said. "Your city is falling apart."

"I think we're doing just fine," Cain said coldly. "I think it's you that's falling apart."
"Maybe I am," I said. "That's why I am going to have to leave this city. I can't be a part of this any longer."

Cain frowned, but remained silent. I turned and walked out of the room.

"Emmanuel," Cain said, as I walked away.

"Yes?"

"I thought we were friends."

"I thought so too."

20

Then she bore again, this time his brother Abel. Now Abel was a keeper of sheep, but Cain was a tiller of the ground.

Genesis 4:2

I went straight home. Sarah was there, putting Nava and Nadir to sleep. I sat down on the bearskin mat Eve had given us, and waited. I meditated silently. I thought over everything that had happened since I had met Adam. I reflected on how much I had grown, what a changed man I had become. I wasn't going to throw everything away because Cain and the people of Enoch had forgotten the values that had made them great. I was going to take Sarah and the kids to a better place and we would start again.

My eyes were closed. I felt the press of soft lips on my forehead. I opened my eyes. Sarah. She was smiling down gently at me.

"Come here," I said. I took her in my arms, and she sat on my lap. I pressed the side of my face against her neck. "We're leaving tomorrow."

"You talked with Cain?" Sarah didn't seem disturbed by the sudden revelation.

"He's become corrupted," I said. "He's worse than the men of the tavern. He's not going to be a leader of mine."

Sarah pressed my hand against her breast and turned her head and kissed me on the cheek. "I told you I'd follow you wherever you go," she said. "Take us to the next stop on our journey. I know you'll do what's best for our kids."

"I want to go see Adam," I said. "I want to tell him about what is happening in Enoch, and ask him to guide me as to where to go next."

"Are we leaving in the morning?"

"Before dawn. We'll take two horses. Nava will ride with me and Nadir will ride with you."

"I'll go get ready."

I awoke an hour before dawn, and woke Sarah. Nava and Nadir were sleeping. Everything was packed and the horses were ready.

"Let's go, Sarah," I said.

"We're not going to say goodbye to anybody?"

"If we're meant to see them again, we will. For now I want to go without any hassle."

"Alright."

We went outside. The air was crisp and chill. A low mist hung beneath the night sky. Stars twinkled and shone up above, and a crescent moon loomed large and deeply yellow.

I helped Sara up on her horse and handed her the baby. Then I climbed onto mine with Nava in my arms.

"Where are we going, daddy?" Nava asked, sleepily. She had awoken when I climbed onto the horse.

"We're going on a journey, to see Adam. Then we're going to live somewhere new."

"Is mommy coming?"

I laughed. "Of course. And Nadir is coming too."

"Okay, daddy."

I smiled. My daughter was so sweet.

I led the way. Sarah followed me. We walked our horses to the edge of the city, then out into the fields and past the river. Then we quickened to a trot and came to the narrow path twisting through the hills. The path we would follow all the way to Adam.

We rode for four days. We had food with us, and we stopped for meals and snacks. At night, we would get off our horses and I would set up a small ox-hide tent for us to sleep in. The weather was fine. We enjoyed the scenery and the change of pace. We would occasionally pick fresh fruits that we didn't usually have in the city and eat them. Nava kept asking questions the whole way, and I patiently answered all of them. Sarah just listened and smiled at her daughter's curiosity.

Finally, after four days, we reached Adam's house. There were tents spread out in the plain, where his soldiers lived. Behind them, there was a garden full of flowers of every kind. A stream flowed gently through it. And behind the garden, surrounded by fruit trees, was a comfortable wooden house. Adam and Eve were sitting on a leopard-skin rug outside their home, enjoying the flowers. They got up when they saw us approach. The men had recognized me and let me pass with only a gentle greeting.

"It's so peaceful," Sarah said. My thoughts exactly. What had immediately struck me about the place was the atmosphere of perfect peace that surrounded it. Gone was the hustle and bustle of the city. Even the soldiers were calm and respectful. An atmosphere of spirituality haloed everything.

Adam and Eve gave us a warm and loving greeting. Eve embraced us both and immediately took Nava from my arms.

"I've missed you, dearest!" she said.

Adam said that we must have had a long journey, and that we should rest a little. Eve led Sarah and the kids inside the house, and Adam walked with me through the garden.

As we walked, Adam told me that the life he desired for his people was easy to talk about, but difficult to practice. He remarked that people follow his teachings for a time, and this leads to great blessings and prosperity; but then when things get easy and the means of enjoyment multiply, people forget their values and the things that brought them success. Then they go the other way and lose everything that had been given to them.

He listened with intent as I related the things that had happened in Enoch. Then I told him that I had left and that I wanted to live with either Abel or Seth. He remarked that I had made a wise choice, because I had a pure heart, and that whoever lives life with a pure heart, even if he makes mistakes, he will be able to correct them and find the right way in the end. I asked Adam if I had made a mistake to go live with Cain. Adam smiled and said that the city has its advantages, but that the country has its advantages too. Perhaps with Abel, he said, I would be able to find the life I so desired for my family. So I should live with Abel and not Seth, I said? Adam replied that I should live with Abel now, and that one day I would experience life in Seth's community as well.

Adam and Eve insisted that we stay with them after our long journey, and we enjoyed their warm hospitality for three days. Nava, who had always been fond of Adam, grew even more attached to him. Adam loved her dearly as well. When it came time for us to leave, Nava didn't want to go, but I promised her that she would see Adam again. So we said our goodbyes to Adam and Eve and headed to the valleys where Abel lived with a community of men and women who herded sheep and cattle.

After traveling for three days, Sarah, Nava, Nadir and I arrived at pastures in a fertile valley where a man was tending sheep. Even from a distance, I recognized him immediately as Heber. He saw us and waved his arms as we approached. A few minutes later, I got off my horse and hugged my old friend.

"It has been so long!" I said.

"You must be tired," Heber said. "I live just over that hill. You must come in and rest."

We followed Heber over a hill, past a small stream, and to his wooden house. Ada was sitting outside, holding an infant in her arms. She got up and waved when she saw us.

"So you're a father now, Heber," I smiled.

"Yes, indeed. Ada is holding my son, Chevron."

I approached Ada and reached out for the child.

"May I?" I asked.

"Of course," Ada said, smiling sweetly. She was nothing like the sly seductress I had first met in the forests of Eden.

I held Chevron in my arms. "A fine boy," I said. "He looks just like his father. And he has his mother's eyes."

"Thank you, Emmanuel," Heber said. He looked serious, graver than when I had seen him last. I handed Chevron back to Ada.

"And you?" I asked my friend. "How have you been?"

"Life is good here," Heber said. "We live in respect for the land and the animals we tend. They provide us with everything, and we offer them our gratitude in return. Abel is a fine leader of our people. We gather every week for a great feast that he puts on to unite the community. He slaughters many animals, and hundreds come, sometimes thousands. On these occasions, he preaches the values that define us as men. Respect for ourselves, each other and the world around us. Harmony with all living things. Our community is thriving. Our women are happy and our children are strong and multiplying."

I was very pleased to hear this. "Things haven't been as good in the city. That's why we left. I just visited Adam and he advised us to come here. Now I can see why. This is a very good place."

"What happened in the city?"

"Let's just say that Cain isn't as responsible a leader as Abel is. Things were getting out of hand. It wasn't turning out to be a good place for families. Men were beginning to forget their values." Heber shook his head. "That's too bad."

I smiled. "Well, we're here now. Say, when's the next feast at Abel's? I'd like to meet him and find a place to settle down." "It is tonight, actually," Heber said. "Ada and I are leaving in about an hour. Why don't you, Sarah and the kids get a little bit of rest, and then we'll all go together? It's only about a twenty minute walk over those hills."

I put my hand around Heber's shoulder. "That would be great, my old friend. It's great to see you again."

21

And the Lord respected Abel and his offering.

Genesis 4:4

When I first saw Abel, the feast was already underway. There were over seven hundred men, women and children picnicking on his property, sitting in the fields amidst the flowers and grasses, enjoying the roast lamb that Abel had prepared and socializing peacefully. I recognized a number of old friends from among the faces there, and then I saw Abel standing outside a graceful wooden house and conversing with a number of men. He saw me as well, and came out to greet me and my family. I introduced my baby son, Nadir, and he introduced his wife, Berura.

"So you decided to trade the chaos of the city for the simple life of the countryside," Abel said affectionately.

"I was working as a metal-smith and prospering greatly at my job," I replied, "but men started drinking and looking lustfully at women other than their wives. I decided it was time to move my family to a better place."

"Men are good as long as they need to be," Abel replied. "But once they gain prosperity and leisure, they forget the important things. What one does with their leisure time is of the utmost importance. One should always be striving to rise higher, become nobler. In our community, we discuss the things of the spirit in our free time. We drink the delicate waters of the spirit and adorn the realm of the soul."

"What you say is like a breath of fresh air," I said. "In the city, we constantly came up with new technologies to make our lives easier. But for our spirits, the air was stifling, and the space forbidding. No spiritual fragrance was wafted to attract us to the regions of peace and well-being. We were always trying our hardest to do more, make more, achieve more, but inside we were becoming puny and weak. Money was making us selfish, and class was making us prideful. The emphasis on comfort, pleasure and ease made us forget our families and occupy our attention with fleeting fancies."

"Did no one else in the city recognize this? Was it only you who felt displeased with this state of affairs?"

"The people were too distracted by the attractions and pleasures of city life. Wine and music are new diversions and the taverns are filled with dancing and promiscuity. Cain, the city's founder and leader, is all the conscience the people need, and he is leading them in the direction of moral bankruptcy."

Abel shook his head. "My older brother is highly intelligent, but he has always been hotheaded and arrogant. It is just like him to follow our father's teachings as long as it conveniences him, and then to bend the rules to a breaking point. But you, Emmanuel, are not and have never been one to follow blindly in another's footsteps. You have always done things on your own. Indeed, you married Sarah before any of us took wives."

"That same free will has taken me from the city into the countryside, where I hope to raise livestock like you and the others."

"And I am glad you are here," Abel said warmly. "Come, you and your family must be hungry. We have much meat prepared for all of our guests today."

After the feast, I discussed the details of my living arrangements with Abel. He pointed to an area of country near Heber's home where I could live, and said that there were plenty of sheep and cattle roaming wild which I could catch and domesticate for my own use. He even said that Sarah and the kids could stay in his own home while I built my house. The construction took a little over a month. I even dug a well so that we would have an easy supply of fresh water. When the house was finished, Sarah and the kids moved in. Abel helped me catch over a hundred sheep and twice as many cattle, and with the help of several neighbors I built a large wooden fence to enclose them. Three months after I had moved into the countryside, I was ready to begin my new life.

Sarah and the kids loved the new environment. The air was sweet and pure, the sun was always shining, and the hills and valleys were vibrant and serene. Nava especially loved the lambs and calves. I taught her how to milk the sheep and cows, and she would come out with me sometimes as I watched my herds graze in the valleys and meadows. Nava loved nature, and she was always full of questions. "Why are the hills and valleys green? Why is the sky blue? Why does the sun disappear at night? Why can't the sheep talk like we do? Why don't the cattle get angry when we slaughter them for food?" I tried my best to answer all of my daughter's questions, but I also always encouraged her to keep asking them. "You can never have enough knowledge," I would tell her. "You can always learn more and more. There is so much in the world to learn about. If answers filled the world from the earth to the sky, they still couldn't satisfy every question that one could ask."

Nava was two-and-a-half years old now, and Nadir was nearly one. My son could already walk and talk. He was an intelligent, robust, and brave little boy. After coming in from the fields every day, I would prepare dinner and, while waiting for the meat to cook, I would play with Nadir. Often I would wrestle with him, and he would struggle with me long and hard through what must have been to him grueling matches. His intensity and perseverance pleased me greatly. I would often say to Sarah that he would be a great wrestler one day, just as I was. "All the better to protect Nava," Sarah would say.

Heber and Ada would often come over and visit. Their son, Chevron, was slightly older than Nadir, and they made great playmates. Sarah and Ada also became close friends. Heber and I would joke that our old friend, Ebron, would be horrified to see how domesticated and docile we had become. But the example and teachings of Adam had truly changed us. We were new men; men, indeed, for the first time. What we had been before could not have been characterized as manhood. We were boys—wild boys. Manhood requires maturity, strength, responsibility, resolve. Now we had all of these. We cared for and loved our families. We were leaders in our communities.

One day, Ada discovered that she was pregnant. A week later, Sarah realized that she was pregnant too. I was excited to hear the news and looked forward to the arrival of our third child. The simple life we lived in that fertile valley was wholesome and satisfying, and both Sarah and I were content with it. Our herds grew as our sheep and cattle gave birth to many offspring, and with these animals at our disposal we had all of the food and livelihood we needed. We enjoyed the quiet of the countryside and the mystical spirituality that seemed to whisper like a soft breeze through the leaves of the trees. Here there were no perverse or corrupting influences from which we had to worry about shielding our kids. Only friends surrounded us and the community was led by a man who cared about the integrity of his own character and those of the people around him. Abel was a good, kindhearted, wise and noble man.

Every week, Abel would hold a feast, and he would talk to the people, and exhort them, with words such as these: "O people! Live good, pure and holy lives. Human life is for eternity. Our bodies are born into this world, mature, grow old, and die, but our souls live on forever. The home of the soul is the heart. Keep your hearts clean and righteous. Do good to each other. Show kindness, compassion and love. Share of what you have, and if your neighbor needs help, hasten to his assistance. Give time and attention to your children. Teach them all that you know, so that nothing that has been learned is lost. O people! The true life is not the life of the body only, but the life of the spirit! Do you see the fields, meadows, valleys, and hills around you? How they are covered by grasses and flocks of sheep, how the sky is filled with blue and dotted with clouds? How the sun and moon revolve and keep the world illumined? As long as these things last, and longer, your souls will live and endure. You will enjoy the beauty of these natural things both in this life and in the life that comes after death. Learn to appreciate the world that surrounds you, then! Live in communion and harmony with it, achieve unity with it. Appreciate your flocks, your homes, your families. Be content with what you have, because these things assuredly suffice you. You have been given everything you need in this life. Be content, then, with what you have been given. He who wants more is always needy. He who wants only what he has, such a man always has enough. And reflect: what could be more precious to you than your own families, than those who truly love and depend upon you? Return their love, be good to them, care for them. Do not forget your duty to your wives and to your children. Always to love, always to protect. Be present with and available to those that need you. They are the source of your true and lasting joy, and you must be the source of their joy as well. A true man keeps his family joyous and happy. His children grow up confident, strong and secure. His wife feels satisfied and safe. These are the teachings of Adam that I relate unto you and that I want you to remember. This, my people, is how I want you to act."

In my own time, I would walk the hills and valleys with Nava and talk to her to the degree that her young mind could comprehend. "The way a fierce grizzly bear loves her cubs, that is the way I love you, Nava. The way the sun and moon revolve around the earth day and night, that is the way I love you. I want you to note carefully the way I love you, so that you always know that you deserve to be treated this way. You are the most precious and important thing in the world. Everything that I have, I have for your sake. Everything I do, I do it for you. I am your father, Nava. I am here to guide you and protect you. I will always be your best friend. You can depend on me, and trust me. You will always come first in my life. I place your happiness and well-being before my own.

"One day, you will be grown, and you will have a family of your own. When that day comes, you must love your children the way your mother and I have loved you. You will choose a young man from among the people to be your husband. He must be kind, respectful and loving. He must be responsible and trustworthy. He must be enlightened and live in harmony with all the world. With this man, you will build a home. It will be a shelter and sanctuary for your children. Together, you will raise your children to be good, righteous and respectful individuals. You will value them and help them to develop their talents and capacities, just as I value you.

"You are a unique person in this world. There is no one else like you. No one can do the things you can do. No one can become what you can become. You can do great things. You are unbelievably powerful. I want you to know what you are capable of. I want you to take the limits off of yourself. Do you see the sky, how high it is above the valley below? That sky is the limit to what you can achieve. Use your imagination, and dream big dreams. Even the biggest dream will become a reality if you believe. Never doubt yourself, and never falter in your convictions. When you set a goal for yourself, work toward it and persist in that work. Never give up. Be relentless. When you stay the course in anything you set out to do, your end will be attained. Consider nothing impossible of achievement. No ideal is too lofty. Make all of your ideals into reality. I do not know what your destiny is, Nava. Only you can know that. But I know that your destiny is very great, and one day you will attain it.

"Look at what one great man can do. Adam had a dream. He lived in Eden among a dark and primitive people. He believed that he could enlighten them and bring them from ignorance to knowledge, from savagery to righteousness and justice, from darkness to light, from death to life. This one man, singly and alone, did all of this. He found his part to play, and he played it. Now I am here with you, telling you that you can do similar things, and even greater than these. I know this about you because I love you. Love fills our hearts with knowledge and teaches us what we did not know before and what no one could have taught us. The knowledge of love is infallible, perfect, and limitless. In addition to that knowledge, love gives us the faith, the strength, the fortitude and the courage to put it into action. What is the use of having all of the knowledge in the world if we can do nothing about it? Love is the power that gives us the strength to act. Through love, we can overcome all things and endure all trials. Love works miracles, and love is what I have for you. I want you to feel this love, I want you to cherish it and to know it so that for the rest of your life you will be able to draw on the power of love for strength and support. Love, my dear Nava, will solve every difficulty."

22

Am I my brother's keeper?

Genesis 4:9

The months passed quickly as I herded sheep and spent quality time with my family. Soon it was time for Sarah to give birth. It was a girl, my second daughter. We named her Addie.

Abel and his wife Berura were present to welcome Addie into the world.

"You must be very proud," Abel said.

"I'm thrilled to have another beautiful baby girl," I replied.

"Another woman in the family for Emmanuel and Nadir to take care of," Sarah said.

"Both you and Nava are strong women," I said. "I am sure Addie will be one as well. I think you three can take care of yourselves."

"What are you here for then?" Berura asked, amused.

"I'm here to do anything the women of my family need me to do," I replied.

"We need you to be a man," Sarah said. "A strong man."

"The strongest men are the most gentle around those they love," Abel said. "And from what I know of Emmanuel, he is exceedingly loving to his family."

"As are you, Abel," Berura said tenderly.

"Emmanuel is the most loving man in the world to us," Sarah said. "I wouldn't replace him with anyone."

I laughed. "Good," I said. "Because you're the one who insisted on being stuck with me in the first place."

"The woman had good foresight," Abel said. "And it is not difficult to recall how poor yours was in the beginning, Emmanuel."

"It took a war, a violent wrestling match, an unexpected visit from you, and the love and wisdom of Adam himself to bring me to my senses," I said. "But I finally realized what a gem I had in the woman right in front of me."

Sarah rocked Addie in her arms. "And now you have another gem right in front of you. The third little gem we've made together."

I couldn't resist the urge to kiss Sarah. "It's amazing what we've made," I said.

I was now twenty-two years of age, and Sarah was twenty. We were still young, although we had lived so much. I felt happy and joyous to possess the strength of youth as well as the wisdom and maturity of manhood. I credited Adam with helping me to combine the two. Without his help and guidance, I still would have been lost in the wilderness of my passions and corrupt desires.

Two months after Addie was born, I decided to go to the city to buy some supplies for our home on the pasture. I wanted to buy some metal tools for tending Sarah's small garden, knives, pots and pans, and some new clothing. I had sheared the wool off of my sheep and intended to sell it in the city in exchange for the things I wanted. When I informed Heber of my intent to travel, he decided to come with me. He wanted to buy some things too, and he wanted to see the city he had heard so much about. So Heber and I set off on our horses, along with sacks full of wool, and made our way to Enoch.

We rode quickly, and arrived after several days. When we got there, it was near noontime. We went straight to the city headquarters in order to ask Cain where we could sell our wool. However, Cain was not there, and his offices were empty. I wondered where he was at that time of day. We went to the clothmakers next, and they too weren't at their shops. We finally went to the metalsmiths, thinking that we could exchange our wool directly for their goods, and they weren't there either. We were surprised at this, for the city seemed full of people, and there were various individuals walking the streets. We asked several people where Cain, the clothmakers and the metalsmiths were. They shrugged and replied that they were probably at the tavern.

"The tavern that Emmanuel loves so much!" Hebert replied.

The men shrugged and looked at me closely. "Didn't you leave Enoch because you didn't approve of what was going on there?"

"So you remember me correctly," I said. "My friend Heber here was just being facetious."

"Well, I guess that we can go to this tavern now so I can see all the frolicking fun for myself," Heber replied delightedly.

"If you didn't like it before, you certainly won't like it now," one of the men said.

"Why, what are they doing there that they weren't before?" I asked.

But the man didn't reply. "Just go there and you'll find out," another man said. "That way, if it makes you angry, you won't take it out on us."

"What makes you think I'll take anything out on you?" I said.
But the men just shrugged and walked off.

"Apparently people didn't take you leaving Enoch so well," Heber said. "They've probably been telling stories about why you left."

"They didn't want to face the truth about themselves, so they made me into a monster," I said.

"Makes sense."

"Let's go to the tavern."

I led Heber to the tavern I used to frequent when I lived in the city. I knew that was the one that Cain would probably be in as well.
The tavern was full of people, although it was the middle of the day. A number of men were playing the flute and the harp, and women were dancing at the back of the tavern. Naked women, making lewd and provocative movements.

Heber just gawked at the women, unbelieving. I shook him out of his momentary reverie.

"The tavern has its enchantments," I said. "But think about Ada."
Heber snorted. "She's more beautiful than these women, but I've never seen her move like that."

"These women's movements aren't for you to see," I replied. "Let's find Cain."

The tavern was so crowded I couldn't see him from where I was standing, so I moved through the crowd. Men were sitting at tables, drunk and with draughts of wine in their hands, conversing with different women. I knew most of these men. The women weren't their wives.

I finally found Cain in one corner of the room. He was sitting in a comfortable chair, two beautiful women in his lap. Neither of the women was Leila, his wife.

His eyes flashed at me fierce and angry when he first saw me, but then they glossed over and he smiled. "Emmanuel!" he said. "So nice of you to visit us again. And I see you've brought your friend. How wonderful. I am sure you know my friends here? They were with me the last time we met. I think you hurt their feelings a little." The women both smiled at me. "Maybe he's changed, Cain," they said.

Cain laughed. "I know Emmanuel. He's a stubborn fool. Admirable, in a way. So, friend, what's your business?"

"I want to know why everyone is in here when they should be at work," I said.

"It's lunchtime, Emmanuel. We are all on our breaks. Just relaxing before we get back to our tasks."

Somehow I doubted him. "And when will you be getting back?" I asked.

"Whenever we feel like it," Cain replied. "I have some business I have to attend to myself."

"How does this city sustain itself if all you all do is fool around?" I asked.

But Cain just smiled. "The farmers and the miners work hard, of course. But we who have easier jobs, we take advantage of the fact that we can enjoy ourselves."

I raised my eyebrow. "And how do the farmers and the miners feel about that?" I asked.

"It's not up to them," Cain said flatly. "I decided at the beginning that some were worthy of more sophisticated jobs and that some people had to do the meaner work. The farmers, the miners and the herders have their jobs because they weren't smart enough for better work. So I let them put their bodies to good use."

"And you call this making good use of your minds?" I asked, incredulous. "You promised the laborers that you would rotate their jobs in a few years. That way it would be fair."

"Well, I've decided that won't be necessary," Cain said. "People will be keeping their jobs for life."

I looked at Heber, and then I stared at Cain angrily. "You can't do that. You're going back on your word."

"I make the decisions in this city," Cain replied nonchalantly. "I started it. It's named after my son."

"And where is your son now?" I asked. "How would he feel if he saw you with women other than his mother?"

"Relax, Emmanuel," Cain said. "I'm faithful to my wife. We're just relaxing here, that's all. These women have husbands too. We're not sleeping together."

I couldn't believe his hypocrisy. "You're bending all of the rules, Cain. And you're breaking your promises. This isn't going to end well, trust me."

"I do trust you, Emmanuel," Cain replied. Then his tone changed, and he became exceedingly impatient. "I trust you to leave my city immediately. You won't be doing any trading today. Go back to my brother Abel and tell him that I send him my regards."

Cain turned back to the women, who giggled. He stroked the thigh of one and kissed the other on the lips. I doubted that he had never had sex with them.

I turned away, disgusted. "Let's go," I said to Heber.

He followed me through the tavern, towards the door. People turned to stare at me as I walked through. Most of them used to be my friends. Now I couldn't bear to look at them. I felt so disappointed.

When we left the tavern, Heber said, "So are we going?"

I got on my horse, and Heber got onto his. "I want to talk to the farmers and the miners first," I said. "I want to get their side of the story."

We rode away from the city and in the direction of the bronze and iron mines. After fifteen minutes, we arrived at a place where a large tunnel had been dug out of a hill. Heaps of bronze and iron were sitting on piles outside. At either side of the entrance to the tunnel stood a large man with an iron spear.

We got off our horses and walked toward the tunnel.

"What is your business here?" one of the men asked. He looked angry.

"We want to see the mines," I replied.

"The mines are off-limits to all except the miners," the man growled.

"What about you two?" Heber asked. "You don't seem like miners."

"Watch your tongue, boy," the other man said, "Or I'll impale you on the tip of my spear."

"No need to get offended," I replied. "We were just wondering what the two of you are doing here."

The first man snorted. "We are on business of Cain's," he said. "You might as well ask him."

"We've already talked to Cain," I said. "He wasn't very helpful."

"Well then," the second man said. "You'll find that we won't be very helpful, either."

I took a step toward the tunnel entrance, and the men help up their spears threateningly. I stepped back.

"Come on, Emmanuel," Heber said. "These men aren't going to let us in."

We were about to go on our horses when a number of miners came out of the tunnel. Their faces were dirty, their hair and beards unkempt, and their clothes were worn and tattered. They were carrying lumps of bronze and iron, which they carried over to the piles sitting outside.

When one of the men had walked a certain distance from the guards, I approached him.

"Hello," I said. "My name is Emmanuel. You don't look too good, my friend."

The man wiped the sweat off his forehead with a dirty hand. "We are overworked, and underfed," the man said. "Our lives are a living hell. We hardly get to see our families."

I frowned. "Why are you working so hard, when the other people in the city are spending their time resting and having fun?"

"It's not our choice," said another man, who had approached the pile of bronze. "We're forced to work like we do."

I frowned further. "You're forced to work?" I asked.

One of the guards spotted us talking, and he yelled, "Hey, you over there! I told you to leave this place! No talking to the miners!"

"What kind of a rule is that?" I asked. I turned back to the miners. "How are they forcing you?"

"These soldiers here," the man said. "They are loyal to Cain. If we stop working, they'll kill us, and they threatened to kill our families if we complain."

"So they're enslaving you?" I asked. "That's hideous. You're their equals."

"Cain and the higher classes in the city don't view outsiders as their equals. They don't hesitate to take advantage of us."

"You're not outsiders," I protested. "You're members of this city!"

The guard had come up to us, and he pointed his spear at the miners threateningly. "You two," he growled. "Go back to work." The men complied. Then the guard turned to me. "Get out of here, before I kill you," he growled.

The man held his spear a hand's-length away from me. I slowly turned around and called to Heber, "Come on Heber, let's go." Then suddenly, without warning, I turned around, grabbed the man's spear, and yanked it out of his hands. Then I pointed it at him and held it up against his throat.

The man looked at me with wide eyes, alarmed, and held up his hands. "Don't hurt me," he said. "I was only following the orders given to me by Cain."

I pressed the tip of the spear harder against his throat. "You go back to Cain, and tell him that the way he is treating his people is wrong. Tell him that this has to stop."

I kicked the man in the groin and tossed the spear out of reach as he fell to the ground, coughing. Then Heber and I jumped on our horses and rode away.

We stopped at the farmlands to see how the farmers were faring. The farmers were indeed working, but around them were standing more tough-looking men with iron spears.

"Do you want to go talk to the farmers?" Heber asked.

I shook my head. "I've seen enough. This is how Cain is using his technology—enslaving his own people."

"What are we going to do now?" Heber asked.
"There is only one thing we can do," I replied. "We are going to see Adam. He'll know what to do."

As Heber and I talked, several horsemen rode toward us. They were holding spears in their hands. I recognized their leader as the guard from the mines.

"They want to kill us," I said. "Let's go."

Heber and I rode off at a sprint. They chased us for almost an hour, but gradually fell behind and gave up the pursuit.

"It's a four day's ride to Adam's home, three at this pace. Are you ready to ride with me?"

Heber smiled and nodded as the wind blew through his hair. "It's just like old times, Emmanuel," he said.

23

And in the process of time it came to pass that Cain brought an offering of the fruit of the ground to the Lord. Abel also brought the firstborn of his flock and of their fat. And the Lord respected Abel and his offering, but He did not respect Cain and his offering. And Cain was very angry, and his countenance fell.

Genesis 4:3-5

Adam was deeply disappointed to hear the news about what was happening in Enoch. He said that Cain had always struggled controlling his passions. Adam had always given extra attention to his son, in the hopes that he would reform his inner nature. He had counseled Cain long and hard to the end that he might break free from his habits of covetousness and extreme ambition. But, Adam saw, it had all come to no use in the end. Cain had abandoned the path of righteousness in favor of the gratification of his base and carnal desires. The injustice and oppression that was happening in Enoch, Adam knew, was unacceptable. So he came up with a plan to let Cain know about the error of his ways.

Adam decided to send messengers to both Abel and Cain asking them, as his two oldest sons, to send him tributes and offerings from among their goods as a mark of their loyalty and gratitude to their father. Adam knew that Cain was especially eager for his father's approval and affection, and that he would want to please him. Adam invited Heber and me to remain with him as his guests while we waited for Cain and Abel's offerings to arrive. So we stayed in tents spread out in Adam and Eve's lovely and graceful gardens as we waited to see what would transpire between Adam and his sons.

As we waited, Adam shared with us his wisdom and told us many things. He thanked and commended us for being good, brave and honest men and for maintaining our integrity. He said that we had chosen well, because those who turn toward the path of good receive all good and blessedness in return. Nothing is certain in life, Adam said, but the well-being and joy of the heart that comes with making right choices and shunning all evil. What men strive for day and night, with all of their effort and strength, is often the material prosperity, pleasure, ease and comfort in this world that comes and goes like a leaf blowing in the wind. All of the physical good that a man can secure for himself is never really secure at all; and in the end he will lose everything he has striven so hard for and end up in the greatest distress and despair. The only thing that can satisfy a man, Adam said, truly satisfy him, and not appease his appetites one moment and leave him empty and hopeless the next, is the moral life. If a man has his honor and integrity nothing can disturb his peace and composure. The good and righteous man will brave the storms and stress of the world which will only touch the surface of his life while in the depths he will remain calm and serene. The selfish and hypocritical man, however, will be plunged into the depths of anguish and bitter agony the moment one unfortunate circumstance dispels the illusion of serenity which he had attained. Living a selfish and immoral life is the sure way to loss and ultimate extinction, while living a holy life brings every benefit, glory, honor and distinction. If a man does more ill than good in his life, Adam said, it were better had he never lived at all; while if a man becomes a source of goodness, of happiness, of prosperity and peace to his fellow creatures, he becomes immortal and his memory endures forever.

The health of the soul, Adam said, is more important than the health of the body, for the soul is the foundation of human life in both this world and in the world that comes after the body's death. If the body alone is satisfied, while the soul languishes stricken and darkened and near unto death, the good of the body will eventually corrode and disintegrate and a man will be left with nothing. If, however, the soul is blessed, robust and illumined by a life lived in nobility and goodness, then no matter what happens to the body the man will live forever, happy and secure. And it is a sure event that the body will eventually die. A wise man will not put his hopes in a fleeting pleasure and desire, in a life that is surely followed by death, in a sweet cup that is tainted with poison. Bodily comforts and pleasures are like a cup filled with sweet water that is mixed with a drop of poison. One enjoys the draught while he drinks it, but afterwards death swiftly follows. Whereas, the soul never dies, so an investment that builds the good of the soul is one that will return life, light and blessings forever.

Two weeks later, as it happened at the very same hour, Cain and Abel arrived. Abel came from the direction of his pastures, and brought with him a large herd of sheep and cattle. Ten men from his community had come with him, tending the flock and helping Abel in every way. The night before he arrived, Abel had slaughtered a large number of his sheep and had prepared them for a feast dedicated to Adam. He roasted them slowly over a fire and flavored them with salt and spices. The delicious smell of his offering came with him as he, his men and his flocks appeared over the horizon. He told Adam that this humble offering was all he had, for he and his people lived off of the animals he had brought, and he hoped Adam would accept it. Adam was most pleased with Abel and his offering, and he graciously accepted it. He hugged Abel warmly, commended him for his efforts, told him that he was satisfied with his community and his conduct, and conveyed to him the expression of his warmest wishes and most tender regards.

Cain came with a train of over a hundred men, mounted on horseback. They had brought all sorts of goods from the city. They brought boxes of wheat, oats and corn, as well as flour which his people had ground in the mills. He brought jars and jars of wine, which his people had made and aged especially for him. He brought statues and figurines made out of bronze, and a crown made out of a new metal he had found in the mines: gold. The golden crown, made especially for his father, Adam, was studded with gems of ruby and emerald. He brought chairs and tables made out of wood, knives and spears made out of iron. Also made of iron were pots and pans, and a new invention of Adam's: swords. He had brought hundreds of swords for all of Adam's soldiers and guards, while Cain's men, unable to produce more in time, had carried with them their own iron spears. Cain also brought jars, cups and bowls made of clay.

Cain was sure that this prodigious display and offering would please Adam. The lavishness of the materials he had brought as a gift for his father betrayed clearly the need for approval and affection which Adam's eldest son cherished. Adam, however, was not at all pleased with the offering brought by his son. Immediately upon seeing Cain, and being informed of the things with which Cain hoped to earn his esteem and approval, Adam severely reprimanded him for the depths of infamy to which his conduct had sunk. By what means, Adam reproved, could Cain justify the slavery and ignominy to which he had subjected his own people? It was clear to Adam that all of the goods which Cain had brought had been produced on the backs, and from the sweat, of these unfortunate people of Enoch. It was corruption that had made the production of these goods possible, not honest and noble effort on Cain's part. It was not material goods Cain was offering, Adam insisted, but the very blood of the farmers and miners who had worked night and day without compensation. And what of the wine which Cain had brought? Did he think to presume that Adam would overlook the fact that the fortunate people living the high life of his city indulged in the drink during the day, when they should have been at work or conducting themselves in a manner conducive to the progress and advancement of their families and society? Was the infidelity and immorality going on in Enoch's taverns something that Cain wanted to hide from his father forever? His father knew well enough what Cain had been up to and the man he had become, and was sorely displeased with him. Adam's verbal chastisement of his son was swift and vehement. Cain stared at the ground and, with bowed head and a dejected posture, he received the words of reprimand which his father showered upon him.

Immediately after his father was done with his speech, Cain lifted his head with a red face and fuming eyes. Directing a look full of hate at his brother Abel, he said, "It is you who has talked to our father and, with your words, prejudiced his mind against me. If it were not for you and these two worms—he flashed a look of contempt at Heber and I—our father would have been pleased with my work and the great progress I have made in my city. I have worked long and hard to make Enoch a place of glory, nobility and advancement, and yet now, because of you, my father does not appreciate any of my efforts at all. And to think that he is, in turn, pleased with you! What have you done? You haven't created a single new tool or material good; you haven't invented a thing. Your people are still backward and primitive as they were before in Eden. Surely you have poisoned our father's mind with you words."

But Abel, returning Cain's gaze with a look full of nobility, dignity and strength, replied: "My dear, misguided brother! Why do you think our father is displeased with you? Can you not look at your own conduct and realize the reason for his attitude towards your offering? Verily, what my father has said is so that you will learn a lesson and change your ways. Now, instead of being admonished, you have turned the situation around and directed your fierce displeasure at me. In truth, it should be directed at no one other than yourself. Are you not the one who has forgotten the teachings your father has repeatedly instilled into your mind, pursued the vain and vanishing things of the world, and enslaved and overburdened your own people? Why will you not be admonished, my brother? Why will you not repent? It behooves you to change your ways, and to free your people from their burden of enslavement. For the privileged of your community, encourage them to dedicate themselves to activities that better their own condition and the condition of their families, not to engage in lewd and contemptible acts."

Cain trembled with fury at his younger brother's noble appeal. "You worthless and ignorant ape!" he screamed. "Do you know who it is you are directing your words to? A man who is infinitely more worthy than yourself."

"If you were more worthy, you would have striven to guide me so that I might follow in your path. But all that stirs within you is your impotent rage at seeing your hypocritical designs so clearly exposed."

Cain yelled like a madman, and charged at Abel. The passionate hatred that raged in his heart for his brother was unmistakable. I personally thought he would try to kill Abel at that very moment, but Abel's men stood forward and formed a wall before him—a wall that Cain was unable to pass. Like a wave crashing against a rock, he charged into the bodies of those men but was instantly pushed backward. Then Adam's powerful voice cried in anger for Cain to stop. The bewildered young man instantly obeyed. Bowing his head, and utterly dejected, he walked back towards his own men, bade them leave the gifts behind, mounted his horse, and led the way back to Enoch.

Once Cain had left, Adam encouraged Able to take the swords Adam had brought and give them to the men of his community. The rage of Cain, Adam warned, remained unabated. The fire of jealousy—jealousy of his brother Abel and his community—burned fiercely in Cain's heart. Adam feared that Abel and his people were in danger. The swords, he said, would be an appropriate measure of defense should Cain and his men attack Abel. Abel, however, insisted that the swords remain with Adam. Adam's soldiers and bodyguard needed to be properly armed. Without the weapons, Adam could not maintain and enforce his authority over the peoples of Earth. Abel assured Adam that he would be able to take care of himself. He did not fear Cain nor his machinations. He was a man—the people of his community were men—and they could take care of themselves.

Abel, his men, Heber and I stayed with Adam and Eve for another day. We enjoyed the feast that Abel had prepared and talked deep into the night. Despite Cain's tantrum and manifest bitterness, we were cheerful and spirited. Being in the presence of Adam inspired infinite joy and confidence. While he spoke to us and walked amongst us, we knew that the world and its problems were but a dream, and that the spiritual world which was our true home would always keep its gates open to us. Within its precincts, we were comfortable, firmly situated, and safe.

The next day, Abel left his flocks with Adam, we all got on horses, and rode away toward our pastures. Abel rode in front, Heber and I rode behind him, and Abel's men took the rear. We were unsure what Cain was going to do, but Adam's warning stood tall in our minds. It did not seem that Cain would repent or mend his ways. He had no sense of shame or remorse for his actions. He had only his jealousy of Abel, the brother whose offering had been accepted by his father to the exclusion of Cain's own. We had all experienced in Eden the horror and violence that jealousy and similar passions such as anger and hate could unleash in the world. We were confident and in our hearts we were calm, but we prepared for the worst.

24

Now Cain talked with Abel his brother; and it came to pass, when they were in the field, that Cain rose up against Abel his brother and killed him.

Genesis 4:8

Things were quiet for about a month. To all apparent seeming, Cain and his people had gone back to the affairs of the city, and had forgotten about the incident with the offering. But in response to Adam's warning, Abel had appointed scouts to watch the borders of his land, and to warn him at the first sign of danger or trouble from Cain.

The weather was calm and temperate, our flocks prospered, and I was able to tend to them for a few hours and spend the rest of my time with my family. Addie was so beautiful and she, along with her older sister and brother, were the pride and joy of my life. I would hold my youngest daughter in my arms and stroll with her over the countryside. I would just talk to her, telling her about the world and herself and the bright future I envisioned for her. "You don't understand me now, darling," I would say affectionately, "but you will one day. You will understand everything one day."
Sarah and I would take the kids out into the meadows around our home, meadows where all kinds of wild flowers blossomed, and picnic with Heber and Ada. Some afternoons we would leave the kids with Ada and strike out on our own, walking through the valleys and over the hills, under the tender sky and joyous sun, holding hands and looking toward the future. We didn't know what the future would bring, but we were excited and full of hope. Sarah was more than my companion and my best friend. She was more than my lover and my wife. She was my heart and soul. We were still young, very young. We had all our lives ahead of us. And, as Adam taught, we had all eternity to look forward to. Together.

"How is it," I asked Sarah on one of these walks, "that I was blessed with the love of the best woman in the world?"

"Good things come to those who deserve them," Sarah replied cheerfully.

"But that's just the thing," I said, "I don't deserve it. I don't deserve you."

"Sure you do, Emmanuel," Sarah said.

"Don't you remember who I was, Sarah? I fought your family just to avoid you. I cared only about myself."

"I fell in love with the man you were," Sarah replied. "And I'm even more in love with the man you've become."

"I am who I am because of Adam," I said. "He was the force that raised me up from my fallen and degraded state. He was the one who educated, guided and taught me. He filled me with his love, and with love for you. I owe everything to him. And, sometimes, I wonder if I owe everything to you, too."

"We owe everything to each other, Emmanuel," Sarah said. "That's the nature of love. And look at what you've done, the choices you've made. You left Enoch when it became unfriendly there. You helped Adam confront Cain about the way he's leading his people. You brought your family to a better place, here with Abel. Every choice you've made has been the right one. That's why you deserve me."
I stood still, and Sarah stopped and turned toward me. I gazed into her eyes. She returned my gaze with tenderness and longing. I raised my hand and touched her cheek. I lifted her chin towards my face and kissed her gently. I put my hand around the small of her back and I felt her trembling. I picked her up and took her to the shade of some trees, where I lay her down and kissed her again. As evening approached, in the cool and tranquil air of the meadow, and laying on a bed of flowers, we made love.

I woke up as the last streaks of sunlight fell sharply upon my face. Sarah was sleeping peacefully in my arms. A number of butterflies were fluttering above us, and a deer and her calf were grazing nearby. I kissed my wife on the forehead and gently woke her. She buried her face in my chest and held me tight.

"Darling," I whispered. "We have to go."

Sarah breathed and continued to snuggle.

"The kids will be fine with Ada, and Heber was going to return early today. We still have a few hours."

I kissed her on the cheek. "It's not that. It's just... I have a feeling. I think we have to get back."

Sarah raised her head and looked at me curiously. "What kind of feeling?" she asked.

I sat up and Sarah sat up as well. "I feel like something's wrong," I said. "I don't want you to worry, but we should get back to the kids." Sarah smiled and put her clothes back on. "Okay," she said.

"Did you know you're beautiful?" I asked her.

"That's what you tell me."

"And your love? It's better every time."

"Eve told me love grows with time," Sarah replied. "She told me she's loved Adam more every day since they first fell in love, and that it would be the same with me."

"Love is a wonderful thing," I replied. "I don't believe there's any greater wealth in the world. And whatever poor soul doesn't have it, that soul is truly deprived."

We walked, arm in arm, back to Heber's home. When we arrived, we found Heber standing outside, two spears in his hand. He tossed me one and motioned for us to come inside.

"Heber, what's going on?" I asked as soon as we entered. The kids were sitting with Ada, who looked concerned.

"We received a message from Abel," Heber replied. "It looks like Cain and a large number of his men are coming, armed with iron spears and swords. Abel feels that Cain is going to attack us. He has called for everyone to gather around his home, where we will mount a defense."

"With wooden spears?" I asked. "What kind of a defense will we be able to mount against weapons like that?"

"Abel has sent for Adam and his men," Heber replied calmly. "But it will take some time. We have to hold Cain off until Adam arrives."

I looked at Sarah. I tried to appear confident and strong, so that she wouldn't worry, but I was afraid for her and the kids. I didn't want anything to happen to them.

"We have to go," I said.

Sarah picked up Addie, I took Nava and Nadir in my arms, Ada took Chevron, Heber carried our spears, and we set out for Abel's pastures. The moon was out, it was full and large, and its light illumined our path. When we made it there, we found thousands of men, women and children— all of Abel's people—gathered.

"Emmanuel, the men look like they're ready for a fight. You go join them. I'll take the kids and go join the women."

I shook my head. "No, Sarah. I'm not letting you out of my sight. You're staying with me."

"But that's not what everyone else is doing," Sarah replied.

"You're not everyone, Sarah. I am going to protect my family. I'm not leaving you."

I spotted Abel, and I led Sarah and the kids over to where he was standing with his wife, Berura.

Abel was holding several spears, with ends made out of sharpened rock, and he handed me one.

"I've had my men make as many of these as we could over the past month," Abel told me. "I knew this day would come."

"Your own brother," I said, exasperated. "How could he do this to you?"

"Pride and stupidity have gotten the better of him," Abel replied. "Leadership, I think, has gotten to his head. He can't stand the fact that I am acceptable to Adam, while he and his city are not."

"Cain was supposed to be part of the solution to Eden's problems," I replied. "But now he's the one who's bringing the worst of those problems back to Earth: violence."

Abel looked steadfastly into my eyes. "I won't survive this, Emmanuel. But you will. Once this is over, you and your family will go to live with Seth and his people. Remember me when you are there. Remember everything I have taught you."

A strange enthusiasm glowed in his eyes. Looking at him, and hearing those words, I felt choked with sadness and tears came to my eyes. "Abel," I replied. "You are a good man. A great man. I do not want anything to befall you."

"Nothing can befall us but what God has ordained for us," Abel replied.

"What?" I asked, confused. I had no idea what he was talking about.

"A teachings of Adam's, secret until now," Abel replied. "We were going to enlighten the people about God as soon as they were ready. Now it is for Seth to inform you of such mysteries. As for me, the time has come for me to move on."

I gripped the spear tightly in my hand. "I won't let you die," I said. "The time of my death is not for you to decide," Abel replied. "For each of us, there is an appointed time. Nothing that can be done, for either good or ill, can hasten or retard that time for even a moment. Trust in yourself, Emmanuel, and protect your family. They are your responsibility, not I."

Abel embraced me, and then walked to the top of a hill, where he observed the horizon with his leading men. I shepherded Sarah, who was holding Nadir and Addie and to whose leg Nava was clinging, further behind the women and children.

"With this spear," I told Sarah confidently, "I will kill any man who tries to hurt you. None of us will die this day."

"Emmanuel," Sarah said, "Go and fight with the other men. If your line breaks, come back for us. We will be here."

"Sarah, I don't want to leave you," I replied. "Who will protect you if I can't find you?"

"Trust, Emmanuel," Sarah replied. "Have faith in us. Go now, and man the front of the line. Your people need you."

I gave Sarah a kiss, hugged Nava, and told them to stay beside a certain tree which was standing nearby. "Do not leave this spot," I said, "And at the first sign of trouble, I will come here to fetch you." I went to the front of the line of men, forming across the hills and pastures around Abel's home. Abel had returned with the intelligence that Cain and his men were just across the horizon. He was mounted, as were one hundred of his men. A man, sent by Abel, offered me a horse, but I opted to stand and fight with the rest of the men on foot.

"Give it to another man," I said, "Who needs it. Abel has informed me that I will survive this grievous day. Standing on my own two feet, and with this spear in my hand, I will slay all who fight us as prompted by their own base instincts of passion, jealousy, hatred and greed."

I saw Heber mounted on one of the horses, a spear in each hand. He nodded to me, and I nodded back.

Soon thereafter, I could hear the shouts of over fifteen hundred men, led by Cain, who had come to attack us. A large number of them were mounted and carrying torches, followed by a furious army on foot. Each of the horsemen had a heavy iron spear in hand, and the footmen carried both swords and spears.

"These men are disciplined and heavily armed," Abel shouted to his men, as he rode back and forth the front of the line on his horse. "Be fearless, and do not falter. Most of us will die today, but we will die with honor. Remember what I have striven so long and hard to teach you. Character is the truest strength of man. Stand firm and steadfast, maintain your courage and enthusiasm, and even bodily defeat will be unable to bring shame upon your souls."

Cain's army was now drawing close. "For our families!" I shouted. "For our families!" came the reverberating reply from the men. I stood braced and ready for the battle that was coming. As the opposing army neared, I could see Cain at the front of his men, riding on a massive horse, a sword in each hand.

"Abel!" he shouted. "Abel!"

"My time has come, my friends," Abel said to us calmly. "I will see you all again in the afterlife, in a place much better than this."

He rode forward alone, motioning for his men to keep the line. Cain's army stopped as well, and he advanced, alone, against his brother. The two rode at each other, Abel with a spear in each hand, Cain with a sword in each of his. I braced myself to see the result of the impact of the two brothers, sure that Cain would inflict a staggering wound to his brother with his swords, each of which, I could now clearly see, was adorned with a hilt of gold studded with rubies.

But it was Abel who struck first. He hurled his spear at Cain with all his strength and found his mark. Cain was pierced through the shoulder and, screaming in rage and pain, dropped the sword from the wounded arm. Abel, perceiving his brother to have momentarily dropped his guard, leaped from his horse and knocked Cain to the ground. In the struggle that ensued, both Cain and Abel dropped their remaining weapons and rained blows upon each other with their bare fists. The men of Enoch, perceiving that Abel had the advantage over their beloved leader, charged towards us. Eager to defend the great man who led our own community, we, too, in turn, charged. In the commotion that ensued, I lost track of the two brothers and eagerly found my own target from amongst the men of Enoch.

The cavalry met each other first, and horses and men fell in an orgy of slaughter. From what I could see from my position amongst the men, the horsemen of Enoch both outnumbered and outfought our own. The iron spears felled horses and men, who tried their best to return the assault with equivalent ferocity. Soon thereafter, I and the other men had joined the fight. I launched my spear at a horseman, who was hit in the stomach and who fell off his horse in a shower of blood. I picked up his spear, a long, heavy iron one, and used it to fell a horse that was fast charging at me. The horse stumbled to its knees, and the rider dismounted, landing on his feet and rushing at me with a glittering sword. A spear from one of my fellows hit him in the neck and felled him instantly. I rushed forward to the spot and, picking up his sword, scanned the crowd eagerly for a sign of Abel. He was our best fighter and our best chance for success, while Cain was the best fighter for the foe. I soon found, to my dismay, that, amidst the wild carnage that surrounded them, Cain and Abel were still facing each other, Abel on his knees and bleeding profusely, Cain standing over him with a sword to his neck. I rushed forward to Abel's assistance. As I drew near, I could hear Abel saying, in grieved tones, to Cain, "Had you done well, God would have accepted you, my brother. But you have, of your own will, done wrong to both your people and to mine. Sin now lies at the door." Cain stood before his brother, trembling. Hot-tempered as I knew he was, I was surprised by his apparent self-control. His face was red and his eyes flashed with fury.

"Will you not beg for your life, you self-righteous and contemptible coward?" Cain asked.

Abel looked at him gravely. "I will not survive the wounds you have already inflicted upon me. Hasten, and finish your deed."

"No!" I shouted. I knocked Cain off his feet and threw him to the ground. I was about to strike off his head with my sword when, at the last second, I hesitated. I did not want to kill a son of Adam. Instead, I punched him in the shoulder and he screamed in pain. I then kneed him in the groin, as he had done to me in our wrestling match all that time ago, and then I punched him several times in the face. Stunned and exasperated, he fell unconscious to the ground. I ran over to Abel, who had been slashed in the chest, side and leg with Cain's sword. He was nearly unconscious for the loss of blood. I held him in my arms as he began to faint before me. He tried to speak, but he only coughed, blood spurting from his mouth. Tears flowing down my face, I felt the last breath expire from his trembling frame. Abel, the noble son of Adam, was dead.

I looked at the wild battle waging furiously around me. A man had helped Cain back onto his horse, and had led him away from the front of the battle. Then I realized with a pang of fear that our line had been broken. With their superior weapons, the people of Enoch were winning the battle in spite of the fact that we were clearly the braver and stronger fighters. I did not know what fate had befallen Heber, but I rushed back to the spot where I had told my family to wait. There was nothing left to do but to retreat, with them, to safety.

25

And He said, "What have you done? The voice of your brother's blood cries out to Me from the ground. So now you are cursed from the earth, which has opened its mouth to receive your brother's blood from your hand. When you till the ground, it shall no longer yield its strength to you. A fugitive and a vagabond you shall be on the earth."

Genesis 4:10-12

As I sprinted back through the crowd of fallen and struggling men, I spotted an unmanned horse and leaped onto the saddle. I spurred it onward toward the crowd of women and children who were standing, apprehensively, and watching their husbands, brothers and fathers die at the hands of the men of Enoch. I leaped off my horse, grabbed the bridle and led it to the tree where I had told Sarah to wait. She was still there, holding the children and speaking to them calmly to try to alleviate the fears inspired by the shouting and screams of men, shouts and screams which were piercing the darkness of the night.

Sarah smiled when she saw me. She looked serene and confident, assured that no harm would befall me or her children.

"I've been waiting for you, Emmanuel," she said. "Is it time to go?"

"Abel has fallen," I replied. "The battle is lost."

"What about these women and children?" Sarah asked. "What will befall them?"

"We cannot stay around to find out," I told Sarah. "I need to keep you and the children safe."

"I don't think it's right to leave them, Emmanuel," Sarah replied. I sighed. "Where's Ada?" I asked.

Sarah pointed to where Ada was waiting, with Chevron, for Heber to return. I ran and fetched her.

"I want the two of you to get on this horse and ride until you find Seth," I replied. "You will be safe with him. If I survive this, I will find you. If not, tell Seth that my dying wish is for him to take care of you."

"You won't die, Emmanuel," Sarah said. She said it matter-of-factly and with complete confidence. I smiled at my wife's intrepidity and helped her onto the horse. I helped Ada on behind her and handed the children up to them. Taking the reigns, Sarah told me she'd see me again soon, and rode off into the night. I turned my eyes back toward the sounds of the battle. Suddenly I heard a woman scream in terror. Cain's men had reached the women and children.

I sprinted toward the sound of the scream and saw several bloodthirsty men, wild with rage, hacking wildly at defenseless women and children. I picked up a rock and smashed in the head of one of the men from behind. Falling to the ground, he dropped his sword, which I picked up. Then I turned to face the other attacker. Grinning like a madman, his face, chest and arms covered in blood, he came at me with his sword. I swung at him and our swords met in the air. We drew them back and they clashed again. This time, I pushed mine forward and slashed him across the thigh. He stumbled, and I thrust my sword into his chest. Still grinning insensibly, he fell to the ground, blood spilling from his mouth.

It was too little, too late, however. More men had come. I faced them courageously, but they outnumbered me ten to one. And more were coming. Two of them stepped forward. I struck one of them on the leg, but the other sliced me across the left arm. I turned and slashed that men across the chest, and the first man thrust his sword into my thigh. I fell to one knee and, with a scream, struck off his head. Then I twisted to avoid the other man's sword thrust, grabbed his hand and pulled the sword from his grasp. A sword in each hand, I stabbed them both into the man's chest. I had not yet pulled the swords out of my dead opponent when a spear struck me through the back and came out through my side. I fell to the ground, staggered. In a flood of pain, I felt the man pull the spear out of me, and he rolled me onto my back. I looked up at him as he brandished his sword before me. I felt sure that he would deal his finishing blow when more shouts came.

"Adam!" a man shouted. "Adam is here!"

The man looked up in shame and fear. Then I heard Adam's unmistakable voice raised above the clamor of the battle. All other shouts ceased as he spoke. Friend and foe alike listened, frozen, to his words. He remonstrated the men of Enoch for their attack and informed them about the dastardliness and shame of their conduct. The men standing over me dropped their swords and bowed their heads in disgrace. They listened, with feelings of remorse and despondency, to Adam's verbal chastisement. Then I felt a gentle hand on my arm. It was Eve. Her radiant face exhilarated my heart and restored a measure of strength to my fading limbs.

"Sleep," Eve said, "You are hurt, but fear not. I will heal you and enable you to return to your wife, who eagerly awaits you."

As if in response to her command, I felt exceedingly tired and a heavy sleep came over me. I closed my eyes and drifted off into darkness.

When I awoke again, I felt a throbbing pain in my back and side. My arm, leg, and torso were covered in bandages. I was indoors, but light streamed in from the window to my room. I looked around, and realized that I lay on a bed. I didn't know how long I had been passed out.

As if on cue, Sarah entered the room. She smiled in joy when she saw me looking at her.

"You're awake!" she said. "You fought so bravely."

"Thank God you're alright," I replied. "What happened?"

"Adam and Eve arrived, with their soldiers, just before the men of Enoch killed the women and children," Sarah replied. I was standing off at some distance on my horse when I heard the sound of Adam's voice commanding the people to lay down their arms. I knew that they would instantly obey, and that all was safe, so I returned. When I did, I found Eve bent over you, applying balm to your wounds. I was momentarily distressed at the sight of the blood that covered you, but Eve assured me that you would be fine, and that we were destined to live a long and happy life together in the lands of her youngest son, Seth."

I shook my head. "Where are we now?" I asked.

"Abel's house," Sarah replied. "Adam and Eve buried him yesterday, along with all of the other fallen men. Most of Abel's men are dead, and more than half of Cain's."

"What will become of the women and children?" I asked.

"Some of them will join Seth's people," Sara said, "And some will return with Adam and Eve, to live under their protection."

"And what of Cain?"

"He had left the battle, as he was wounded in several places, but Adam's soldiers found him and brought him back to his father. 'What have you done?' Adam asked his son. 'The voice of your brother's blood cries out to me from the ground. So now you are cursed from the earth, which has opened its mouth to receive your brother's blood from your hand. When you till the ground, it shall no longer yield its strength to you. A fugitive and a vagabond you shall be on the earth.'"

"So Adam banished Cain from the land?" I asked.

"With the rest of his men, and their wives and children," Sarah said.

"Cain was afraid and exceedingly sorrowful. 'My punishment is greater than I can bear!' he said. 'Surely you have driven me out this day from the face of the ground; I shall be hidden from your face; I shall be a fugitive and a vagabond on the earth, and it happens that anyone who finds me will kill me.'"

I shook my head. "I don't know what that proud and irresponsible man was thinking," I said. "Did he not think, when he rose up against his father, that he would incur his father's fierce displeasure? He has brought this drastic punishment upon himself."

"Adam was sure that Cain would be fine," Sarah replied. "He has his swords and his smarts. But he will have to build the city of Enoch somewhere else."

"How far a man can fall," I sighed. I sat up. Sarah rushed over to me, and eased me onto my back. "Not yet," she said softly. "But Eve said that you will be back to walking in a few weeks."

"That man," I said. "He stabbed me through the back. How did I survive?"

"After Cain and his men left, Adam put his hand over your wounds and stopped the bleeding. Then Eve made an ointment and spread it over your wounds, wrapped you in bandages, and asked her men to carry you here."

Suddenly I remembered that I didn't know what had happened to my best friend. "Heber," I said. "Is he alright?"

Sarah smiled compassionately and put her hand over mine. "He didn't make it, Emmanuel," she said softly. "I'm so sorry. Ada and Chevron were devastated."

I felt like the breath had been knocked out of me. I didn't know what to say. I felt like choking. My heart sank.

Sarah kissed me on the forehead. "I'm sorry, Emmanuel," she repeated.

"These terrible wars," I said, exhausted. "When will they end?"

Sara looked at me tenderly. "You need to rest. Ease your mind. The wars are over for now."

"For now," I said. Then I closed my eyes.

"Sarah," I said, as I drifted off to sleep."

"Yes?"

"Stay by my side."

"I'll be right here."

When I woke up again, Sarah was still there, and so was Eve. Their radiant faces brought me joy as soon as I opened my eyes. "The two most beautiful women in the world," I said cheerfully. "I wish I didn't have to lie here, helpless like this, while you two wait on me." Eve smiled. "You'll be up and walking soon," she said. "You're already much better, and it's only been a few days."

"I heard you and Adam healed me," I said. "Thank you."

Eve looked at me tenderly, and suddenly tears came to her eyes. "Thank you for sparing my son's life," she said.

I didn't know what she meant. "I thought Abel died," I said, confused.

"Abel died, but Cain lived," Eve said. "Adam had to banish him from the land, and I will never see him again, but I am glad that he's alive. His life will be hard and he will be afflicted with troubles, but he is strong. And despite all that he's done, I love him."

"I am sure Adam still loves him too," I said.

"He does, even more than I do," Eve replied. "Banishing him was very hard, but my husband had no choice. Cain's transgressions had gone too far."

I looked at Eve steadfastly. A question burned inside of me, and I decided to ask it. "How is it, Eve, that Adam's own son—your own son—has done such a thing? Of all people, he should have been the last to act in such a way, and to fall so far."

"He is our son, yes, but he is still a man," Eve replied. "Adam and I taught him everything we could, but we couldn't take away his free will. Had he done well, he would have been accepted, but since he did not do well, sin lay at the door. Sin always desires a man, but he should rule over it."

I said no more. There was nothing more to say. What had transpired was a tragedy from beginning to end. The finest men in the world, in my eyes, had died in an orgy of senseless violence. Overcome by emotion herself, Eve bade Sarah tend to me carefully, and left our presence. A few minutes later, Adam himself came into the room, and addressed to me words of cheer and comfort. He lauded my conduct, courage, bravery, and skill, and instructed me to find Seth. His youngest son, Adam assured me, had reserved a place for me in his community, a place of honor beside himself. He urged me to accept it, and told me that my journey through life had only begun. He then tenderly embraced Sarah, kissed Nava, and left us in the care of God.

After he left, Sarah looked at me curiously. "Who is God?" she asked.

"I don't know," I said. "Abel said that Seth would show us."

"He sounds good," Sarah replied.

"I'm sure he is," I said.

26

And Adam knew his wife again, and she bore a son and named him Seth, "For God has appointed another seed for me instead of Abel, whom Cain killed."

And as for Seth, to him a son was born; and he named him E'nosh.

Then men began to call on the name of the Lord.

Genesis 4:25-26

Under Sarah's care, and with the ointments that Eve had left behind, I healed quickly. Two more weeks, and I was out of bed. A week after that, and I was out and about. Within a month of my injury, I felt as normal and healthy as ever. So I got on a horse, Sarah got on hers, we took our kids, and struck off to find Seth and his farmlands in the country.

We rode five days and on the sixth arrived at the edge of the lands occupied by Seth's community. The people at the first farm we encountered were old friends from Eden, and they greeted us and gave us lunch. Then they pointed the way to Seth's farm. We rode for two hours and we were there.

Seth came out to greet us, and he introduced his beautiful wife, Nina, and his infant son, Enosh.

"My father told me you'd be coming," Seth said warmly. "I had some men prepare a house and some farmland for you. Everything is prepared. Your home is adjacent to ours, and until your crops are ready for harvest, you will eat at our table."

"I don't know how to thank you, Seth," I said.

"Don't," Seth replied. "It is I who should thank you. My mother told me what you did for my brothers—both of them. I am only sorry that I couldn't join the fight."

"It is better that you didn't," I replied. "I wouldn't want another one of Adam's sons killed. Even my survival was a miracle—I was healed by Adam, and your mother nursed me back to health."

Seth looked at my kids. "They're so beautiful!" he said.

"As is yours," I smiled. "Remember when you visited Sarah and me, all that time ago?"

"Yes, Emmanuel, I remember it very clearly," Seth said. "You two were married before anybody else, even before me. Back then, we had dreams of a new society, and the establishment of the family unit as its fundamental building block. Well, that has all happened." Seth looked suddenly sad, and he stared at the ground. "Even with— the setbacks we've had."

I put a hand on Seth's shoulder and tried to encourage him. "What happened with Cain and Enoch was a tragedy, and even more so what happened to Abel and his people. But you are a son of Adam, Seth. You can lead us into a new and glorious future."

Seth looked into my eyes, and I could see a fire glowing in them. I smiled.

"My father has placed that responsibility upon me," Seth said, "and I shall begin by calling upon the name of God."

"Abel's last words to me were that you would tell me about God— that all of our hopes depended upon him—and Adam spoke of God as well. I beg you, Seth, relieve me of my perplexity. Who is this God?"

Seth looked at me steadfastly. "Come, Emmanuel, let me show you your home. We will speak of this more tonight."

That night, Seth had his whole community over at his home. He had spread tents for people to stay in for the night, and we had a great feast. After dinner, I was sitting next to Sarah and the kids as Seth stood before the thousands of men, women and children who had come, and he prepared to speak.

"People of Earth!" Seth called out in a loud voice. "I have a story to tell. Please listen to what I have to say, for these words will be passed down and repeated for unseen generations down all the reaches of time."

I held Sarah in my arms and rested my chin on her head. She squeezed my hands, turned her face and kissed me on the cheek. The people were dead silent as they listened to Seth's words with rapt attention. Only the chirping of the crickets could be heard beneath Seth's loud voice, rising and falling as the handsome young man spoke.

"In the beginning God created the heaven and the earth.

And the earth was without form, and void; and darkness WAS upon the face of the deep. And the Spirit of God moved upon the face of the waters.

And God said, Let there be light: and there was light.

And God saw the light, that IT WAS good: and God divided the light from the darkness.

And God called the light Day, and the darkness he called Night. And the evening and the morning were the first day.

And God said, Let there be a firmament in the midst of the waters, and let it divide the waters from the waters.

And God made the firmament, and divided the waters which WERE under the firmament from the waters which WERE above the firmament: and it was so.

And God called the firmament Heaven. And the evening and the morning were the second day.

And God said, Let the waters under the heaven be gathered together unto one place, and let the dry LAND appear: and it was so.

And God called the dry LAND Earth; and the gathering together of the waters called he Seas: and God saw that IT WAS good.

And God said, Let the earth bring forth grass, the herb yielding seed, AND the fruit tree yielding fruit after his kind, whose seed IS in itself, upon the earth: and it was so.

And the earth brought forth grass, AND herb yielding seed after his kind, and the tree yielding fruit, whose seed WAS in itself, after his kind: and God saw that IT WAS good.

And the evening and the morning were the third day.

And God said, Let there be lights in the firmament of the heaven to divide the day from the night; and let them be for signs, and for seasons, and for days, and years:

And let them be for lights in the firmament of the heaven to give light upon the earth: and it was so.

And God made two great lights; the greater light to rule the day, and the lesser light to rule the night: HE MADE the stars also.

And God set them in the firmament of the heaven to give light upon the earth,

And to rule over the day and over the night, and to divide the light from the darkness: and God saw that IT WAS good.

And the evening and the morning were the fourth day.

And God said, Let the waters bring forth abundantly the moving creature that hath life, and fowl THAT may fly above the earth in the open firmament of heaven.

And God created great whales, and every living creature that moveth, which the waters brought forth abundantly, after their kind, and every winged fowl after his kind: and God saw that IT WAS good.

And God blessed them, saying, Be fruitful, and multiply, and fill the waters in the seas, and let fowl multiply in the earth.

And the evening and the morning were the fifth day.

And God said, Let the earth bring forth the living creature after his kind, cattle, and creeping thing, and beast of the earth after his kind: and it was so.

And God made the beast of the earth after his kind, and cattle after their kind, and every thing that creepeth upon the earth after his kind: and God saw that IT WAS good.

And God said, Let us make man in our image, after our likeness: and let them have dominion over the fish of the sea, and over the fowl of the air, and over the cattle, and over all the earth, and over every creeping thing that creepeth upon the earth.

So God created man in his OWN image, in the image of God created he him; male and female created he them.

And God blessed them, and God said unto them, Be fruitful, and multiply, and replenish the earth, and subdue it: and have dominion over the fish of the sea, and over the fowl of the air, and over every living thing that moveth upon the earth.

And God said, Behold, I have given you every herb bearing seed, which IS upon the face of all the earth, and every tree, in the which IS the fruit of a tree yielding seed; to you it shall be for meat.

And to every beast of the earth, and to every fowl of the air, and to every thing that creepeth upon the earth, wherein THERE IS life, I HAVE GIVEN every green herb for meat: and it was so.

And God saw every thing that he had made, and, behold, IT WAS very good. And the evening and the morning were the sixth day.

Thus the heavens and the earth were finished, and all the host of them.

And on the seventh day God ended his work which he had made; and he rested on the seventh day from all his work which he had made.

And God blessed the seventh day, and sanctified it: because that in it he had rested from all his work which God created and made."

I was still holding Sarah in my arms. "He's a good man, Sarah," I said, "And wise."
"Our children will be good growing up here," Sarah agreed.
I kissed the back of her head, held her tight, and we listened to Seth speak.

The End

www.ingramcontent.com/pod-product-compliance
Lightning Source LLC
Chambersburg PA
CBHW070552130626
46556CB00001B/131